I0571024

UNBRIDLED

*A collection of short stories from
the Alex Crocker series*

Lauren Grimley

No part of this story may be reproduced, stored in a retrieval system, or transmitted, in any form or by any means, without the prior permission in writing of the author, nor be otherwise circulated in any form of binding or cover other than that in which it is published and without a similar condition including this condition being imposed on the subsequent purchaser.

Visit Lauren Grimley's website: www.laurengrimley.com

Note: This is a work of fiction. All characters, places, businesses, and incidents are from the author's imagination. Any resemblance to actual places, people, or events is purely coincidental. Any trademarks mentioned herein are not authorized by the trademark owners and do not in any way mean the work is sponsored by or associated with the trademark owners. Any trademarks used are specifically in a descriptive capacity.

First Edition, Grimm Sisters Publishing

Copyright © 2013 Lauren Grimley

All rights reserved.

ISBN: **0615861113**
ISBN-13: **978-0615861111**

CONTENTS

FORWARD

The Creator, or goddess, in my series created all beings, vampires and humans, males and females, with a balance in mind. I think she'd agree that what women lack biologically in physical strength, we make up for in emotional might, a powerful punch to pack. Yet, too often in fiction, as well as in real life, we're depicted as damsels in distress, as characters in need of saving. It's time we take control of the pens and write our own tales.

Unbridled is about unlikely friendships and less likely lovers. Some parts are dark, others steamy, and still others humorous. Even in its lighter moments though, it's meant to honor all women who have fought the good fight, whether they have survived physical or sexual assaults, abuse, deadly illnesses, or the seemingly more mundane, but still intensely painful experiences of love and loss. Alex may be the first female warrior in my fictional world, but she is preceded by scores of real-life everyday women warriors, who, although they may have been victimized, should never be seen as victims.

Fight on, ladies.

Proceeds from the sale of this book are being donated to two women's charities: The Breast Cancer Research Foundation and V-Day. Please visit the Romance for a Reason page at www.laurengrimley.com for more information.

1. Special Victims Unit: Part 1

Alex stopped dead in her tracks. She spun on Rocky with a taser glare. The stocky warrior stood his ground, but Alex was almost certain he had first shifted a few inches to the right, leaving him an unimpeded fall in case she used her gift to project his vampire ass into oblivion. She was certainly contemplating such a move now that she was close enough to the room she was approaching to sense the emotions of those inside it.

"You said *Sarah* wanted to see me."

"She does." He was subconsciously picking at a scab on his pointer finger with his thumb. A sign he wanted to bite at his nails. A disgusting and obvious tell.

"And the rest of the females in that room?" She should have been suspicious when Rocky had gotten off the elevator at a floor of the club Alex had never needed to go to and headed towards a meeting room she didn't even know existed.

"They want to see you, too."

She raised a brow.

"Okay, Ellie never particularly wants to see you, but I think in this case she made an exception—for your sake, this time, not just to appease Sarah." Ellie was Rocky's girlfriend and had a legitimate reason not to like the Seer. Alex should have been grateful for any sign of concern Ellie showed her. Instead she was pissed.

"So I'm being ambushed." Sarah had hinted at this twice already. Alex had made it clear she wasn't interested.

"Yes, but it's a friendly-fire ambush."

"There's no such thing, Rocky." Alex spun on the heels of her Docs and headed back in the direction they came. Rocky flashed in front of her, a six-foot-two roadblock with fangs. She had gotten over being short long before she entered this world, but she really hated that she was the only one in her life now, aside from her mother, who couldn't move at lightening speed. It left her clenching her fists even tighter.

"I've been given permission by both Sarah and your mate to carry you in there if necessary." He towered over her; his expression teetered between amused and what she assumed was supposed to look intimidating.

Her eyes narrowed at the information that Markus had been involved. She'd deal with him later. "*I* don't need permission to—"

Suddenly she was upside down over his shoulder. Her lunch threatened to reappear. It left her wondering if Rocky dousing the nachos they shared with extra hot sauce had all been part of the ruse.

"Go ahead, Seer, project on me, but be warned, this marble is rough on the skull. I know firsthand from the previous times you've knocked me out with your gift. It would be a nice taste of your own medicine."

"The only thing I taste is bile, so unless you want

your jeans to be the canvas for an intestinal interpretation of a Pollack painting, I'd put me down!" Alex yelped the last word as Rocky began to move at full speed toward the meeting room. She squeezed her eyes shut to keep from being ill.

"Wouldn't be the first time." He flipped her upright just inside the door and shoved a plastic bin that had been on the floor under her chin. When the room stopped spinning, Alex saw the four awaiting females watching her and shoved the wastebasket aside.

"I'm fine. Put it back." She hoped her easily upset stomach would cooperate, so she could maintain some semblance of dignity.

"Thank you, Rocky. We've got it from here." Sarah, the Regan's mate had stood to greet them from one of the couches that lined the sparse but welcoming room.

"Should I stay outsi—"

"No." It was Ellie who snapped a response so sharp it caused Rocky to flinch. When she saw her partner's reaction, she tried to temper it the best way she knew how, by throwing a verbal jab at Alex. "You don't need a machine gun to squash a mosquito." She had flashed to his side and was squeezing one of his 'guns' with a charming grin.

Alex groaned. "I might need that basket after all."

Blushing, Rocky laughed, bowed to Sarah and the other females, and ducked out of the room before Ellie could land the slap she aimed at his rear-end.

"Elizabeth, you gave me your word." Sarah spoke softly enough, but Alex both heard and sensed her frustration. As daughter of a Regan herself, Ellie wasn't accustomed to taking orders, but either Sarah's tone or the somber mood of the rest of the room had her conceding.

"My apologies, Alex. By all means, welcome to the club." Ellie ignored Sarah's exasperated sigh and sulked off to the farthest seat, a leather club chair positioned next to the fireplace. She stared into the flames to avoid the looks of sympathy from the others, Alex supposed. They all knew about the recent events that caused Ellie's mood. Alex's fear was that the related tragedies in her own life were the reason *she* was asked to join.

"Do I at least get to ask what club I'm joining before I decide whether or not I'm staying?"

Vivian streaked to Alex's side. The vampire, tiny for their species, was no bigger than Alex was, but equally as ballsy, though with perhaps more class and charm than Alex ever managed. Alex had liked her immediately when they had met at the Creator's Day party Sarah and the Regan had hosted just weeks ago. Then again, Alex liked any female who gave it back to Sage. As his mate, or as close to a mate as the stubborn Knower would ever agree to, Vivian had perfected the art of torturing him. And others, apparently.

"You're staying, Tinker Bell, so sit, and then I'll answer your question."

"I can tolerate the short jokes and lame height-related nicknames from the over-sized ginger in the corner, but from you?"

Ellie flipped her the bird when Sarah's back was turned. Vivian only smiled. "Sorry. I thought as a counter to Sage's nickname for you, it worked. It *is* better than Twerp. And short or not, I'm still a vampire—and you're not—so sit."

"Please, Alex, just for tonight." Cormelia had been sitting so quietly and still at the end of the couch where Sarah had been that Alex might have missed her if her sense hadn't told her there was one more female present.

Alex's shoulders drooped. How could she say no to the female who had fed her mate for centuries, who had been his confidant and comforter, and pledged to remain so even after he mated a human? Cormelia's loyalty to Markus and her acceptance of Alex held more sway over the Seer than all of Sarah's concern or Vivian's playful threats.

"Fine, but for the record, as a Seer, I can leave at any time. If we're into insect metaphors, dropping vampires like flies is kind of my specialty." At one time or another, they had all seen her project an emotion onto a vampire with such intensity as to render him unconscious. No one denied the strength of her gift, but Sarah did qualify it.

"Except for Leonce." She whispered the words. It was not a taunt or a threat but a reminder of why Alex was there.

"Yeah, well, there's that." Alex sensed no one was fooled by her nonchalance. As a Seer, the one advantage she had over the vampires, both her friends and her foes, was her ability to sense, manipulate, and if needed, to knock one of them out with emotions. It was recently discovered that the one vampire who most wanted to cause her pain, the one who had already caused her the most pain, was also the only one on whom Alex's gift had no effect. When it came to Leonce, she was the fly, and everywhere she turned was another web meant to snag her.

Taking a deep breath, she tried to remember that this newest web cast by her friends was done out of compassion. She let Vivian lead her to the love seat on the opposite side of the fire from where Ellie sat. They had no problem fitting together on the small piece of furniture and, for once, Alex actually welcomed the closeness to another.

When the awkward silence became too much, Alex tried to lighten the mood. "So this club, is it called Girl Time Would Be Good for You? That was Markus's line when Sarah tried to get me here last week. Or maybe you took one from Sage's book and named it Chick Therapy? He's right that it's cheaper than a shrink. Unless the four of you plan to charge me. Do warriors get mental healthcare coverage?"

"You better hope so, because usually there are about a dozen of us, and I can't speak for the rest, but I'm not cheap."

Alex laughed at Vivian's response. Then it struck her. She must have been wrong about what she had been dragged into.

She'd struggled with her emotions since her father's death and the arrival of the photo album the night of her mating ceremony, the one documenting how her family had been picked off one by one at the hands of the Vengatti, the one threatening those loved ones she had left. Unlike when her power first matured, it wasn't her sense of others, but her own spiraling feelings that tortured her. She was angry at what she'd been forced to suffer. She was afraid that she hadn't seen the worst of it. That fear, in turn, made her more furious, because there was little she could do about it. No matter how hard the Regan or Alex's mate tried to protect her, she wasn't willing to stop fighting any more than her mate or friends were willing to stop. The Vengatti knew that. Leonce knew her. He couldn't yet get to her physically, but he'd found a rather effective way to get at her emotionally, which, for a Seer, was saying something.

That she hadn't yet killed or been beaten by her housemates during one of her many temper tantrums was solely due to the fast reaction time of Markus and Sarah.

Lately, though, Alex sensed they were tiring of acting as a buffer zone. They understood the source of her anger and anxiety, and they shared her fear. But they also made it clear in recent nights that they felt she wasn't doing enough to deal with it. Alex had gladly volunteered to 'deal with it' on patrols using her gift and some sharp steel against a few Vengatti scum. That hadn't been what Markus and Sarah had in mind, however. She had been sure when she had been dumped in the room and saw the closest thing she had to a group of girlfriends in the coven, that they had gathered in hopes she'd gush about her emotions in a tearful, estrogen-filled cathartic experience. Vivian's words left her second-guessing that assumption.

"A dozen?"

"Yes. We've had this group meeting once a week for a very long time." Sarah stood behind Alex and squeezed her shoulder reassuringly.

"You mean the world doesn't revolve around Alex?" Ellie had mumbled it, but even lacking the vampires' enhanced hearing, Alex heard.

"You may be stupid, but I'm not deaf, *Princess.*"

Ellie stood up, but Sarah flashed between them.

"Enough. Ellie, if you refuse to even hear Alex's explanation and apology, then you forfeit your right to remain hostile. With that said, Alex, if you are truly sorry, then you ought to have the patience to put up with her raging awhile longer. And both of you need to have the grace not to match each other's comments tit for tat." Sarah paused long enough for both of them to nod. Alex learned early on that the Regan's mate was every bit as formidable and twice as demanding of respect as he was. "Tonight *was* supposed to be all about Alex. That's why only the four of us whom you already know are here. We assumed this would be difficult enough for you without adding the emotions of eight or nine strangers."

Alex didn't comment on the difficulty of being there. Her head was still elsewhere. "I'm confused."

Vivian jumped in to help. "Then let me answer your first question. I'm not sure we ever had an official name, but our newest member, prior to us hijacking your typical Thursday nap in Markus's office—" Alex began to contradict her but was cut off. "Don't deny it. I date the male who spends his life listening to your thoughts. He likes it when you're asleep. Anyway, Ellie cheekily christened us the SVC or Special Victims Club."

Ellie grinned sardonically. "Think *Law and Order SVU* meets *The Breakfast Club*."

Alex was tempted to ask her if, as the only redhead in the room, she was Molly Ringwold. She wanted to know if the lipstick trick was possible. Sarah's position directly in front of her, not to mention the serious meaning behind Ellie's trite explanation, made her rethink it.

"The other females who come each week, they're all of the Vengatti's victims?" she asked instead.

Sarah's sigh sounded like it held the sorrow of centuries. Looking tired and worried, an expression she wore often since learning she was pregnant, she went back to sit next to Cormelia.

Cormelia reached over, held her hand, and answered for her. "We wish that there were only a dozen of us. Other females made the choice to stop attending after awhile or never attended in the first place."

"Is that an option?" Alex's glance darted to the door. Sarah crossed her arms over her chest, resting them on her bulging belly. Alex was being difficult, because arguing about having to be there was easier than talking about the reason they wanted her there. She'd rather they saw her as an argumentative bitch than a victim. She'd rather see herself that way, too.

"You'll have a choice after you've stayed long enough to understand what such a group has to offer."

Alex knew what they had to offer. She'd lived with Elizabeth since she was brought home from weeks of being held captive by the Vengatti. She imagined that the other females' emotions would be just as jarring. She knew others often found comfort learning they weren't alone in feeling what they did. Hearing someone say they felt the same, though, was a far cry from having to feel those emotions layered on her own. Yet that was exactly how Alex's 'gift' worked.

"I'm a Seer, Sarah."

"I know, which is why I didn't bring you here right away. But you've dealt with that challenge. You now have the control to block our emotions if you need to. It's time for you to deal with your own emotions."

Alex balled her hands into fists. "Warriors have our own ways of dealing with things. I don't see any of *them* here. Or Darian. The Regan was attacked that first night, too."

Sarah closed her eyes, either to keep herself from matching Alex's anger or because the reminder of the night she very nearly lost her mate added to her already intense anxiety.

Likely due to centuries of dealing with Sage, Vivian was more comfortable confronting the Seers' snarky response. "You're as much a woman as a warrior. Leonce knew that. His means of attacking you proved it." She reached over and skimmed the tips of her fingers over the scars on Alex's neck that remained from the previous July. Alex stiffened but didn't stop her. Markus was careful, since they started exchanging essence, always to avoid feeding from Alex too close to the marks left from Leonce's attack, but Vivian's small fingers, though cooler, felt almost like her own.

"Darian was bitten in the same spot," Alex continued to argue, though her tone had lost its edge. Vivian drew her hands back into her own lap and countered this too.

"Bitten, to create severe blood loss, but not fed from. The Vengatti never feed from our warriors in a fight. They rarely feed from our males at all. Since our essence encapsulates who we truly are, drinking from it is an act of intimacy. Taking it forcibly is no less a violation than rape. Leonce knew that."

"But *I* didn't know that, not then. To me it was nothing but another battle scar." Alex opened her left hand and stared at a second scar from that night. She remembered the obscene way Ty had licked the blood from the wound, practically purring at the thought of killing her brother before her eyes, the first of many acts of torture he would have inflicted on her had she not escaped. That felt as great a violation as Leonce's bite had.

Sarah must have seen some of that in her expression. "That's the point, Alex. You've been with our coven less than a year and have suffered more injuries, of all kinds, than most of us face in a lifetime."

"Besides," Vivian tugged playfully at the collar of Alex's long-sleeve fitted tee, revealing two tiny new scars above her collarbone. "Thanks to Markus, you now have a very clear understanding of what it all means."

Alex blushed and pushed Vivian's hand away while Sarah and Cormelia both exchanged smiles. Ellie, who had been silently staring at the crackling fire, finally turned to engage with the others.

"I think every vampire from Bristol to the Berkshires

has a clear understanding of the those two's feeding habits. And as if the noise weren't bad enough, I've got to listen to Rocky whining about how the human and her three-hundred-year-old mate have more sex than we do—like it's a competition that will emasculate him entirely if he loses."

Alex and Vivian cracked up. Even Cormelia couldn't hide her smile, but Sarah was once again chastising Ellie for comments unbecoming to a young princess. Ellie's apology didn't help.

"Sorry. I thought talking about sex with our chosen partners was a lighter topic for her first night than informing her that she'd been fang-fucked."

"Elizabeth Jamison!" Baby bump or not, Sarah had shot to her feet.

"That's what the warriors call it. She's supposedly a warrior, right? And we all know I haven't deflowered her virgin ears. At least I wasn't swearing at someone like she usually does."

Alex shrugged. Ellie had a point. And Alex could sense what Sarah could not: Ellie was as uncomfortable being here as Alex. With a pang of guilt she wondered if her presence intensified that discomfort. Alex was both partly to blame for all that Ellie suffered at the hands of the Vengatti and partly to thank for her being rescued. There was no way Ellie could look at her and not be plagued with memories she'd certainly rather forget.

Ellie caught Alex's lingering gaze and misread the reason for it.

"No, I wasn't, in the traditional or vampire way. The Creator spared me that at least. Or Mallory did, if nothing else."

It was back to this. Ellie would never be able to forgive Alex for leaving behind the Vengatti female who had kept her alive during her captivity. It wasn't that Alex hadn't wanted to help Mallory that night. She would gladly have rescued both females had she been able, but she wasn't. She had been forced to make a choice. She chose Ellie, and Ellie had hated her for it ever since.

"I really am sorry. I—"

"Alex." Sarah stopped her. "Not tonight. Not unless she's ready to talk about it."

Ellie didn't look back as she shook her head.

"As you know, Ellie's only been here a few weeks herself. She mostly listens now. We thought that might suit you as well tonight, and beyond, if needed, assuming you'll return."

Alex shrugged noncommittally. She was still withholding judgment about all this, but she was relieved that there was no expectation for her to talk tonight. Although if Ellie wasn't talking either…Alex's eyes darted from Sarah to Vivian to Cormelia. Snippets of their earlier conversations flooded back to her. They had said *us* and *we*. The realization stole the breath from her lungs.

"All of you?" she gasped.

Vivian chuckled grimly. "That took you long enough. And Sage told me you were relatively bright for your kind."

Alex swatted at her as she would have swatted at Sage had he been there. Then she turned questioningly to Sarah.

"Not me. Not directly. But one of my roles as the Regan's mate is to provide opportunities such as this for the coven's females."

"Don't let her fool you, Alex," Cormelia interrupted softly. "Sarah revolutionized her role as the Regan's mate. No other Madame Regan before her has done as much for females as she has, and her compassion, I suspect in ways similar to your gift, means that she suffers nearly as much as we do every time another female walks through that door. And more so when they don't."

Cormelia's assessment of Sarah was so genuine that it took Alex aback. Despite how close they'd grown, Alex had only known Sarah a short time and had rarely seen her interact with others in the coven. Watching the way she handled the males in the house, though, Alex should have suspected Sarah had done plenty over the years to earn the reverence with which others treated her. Unlike the way some coven members acted around Darian or his father, the Elder Regan, this wasn't obedience or fear; it was earned respect.

Sarah smiled back at Cormelia. "Thank you, but it was as much Darian's doing as mine."

It was rude, bordering on dangerous, but Alex couldn't help but scoff. "Am I missing something?"

"About three-thousand years of our recorded history." Sarah's gaze pierced her.

"I'm only interested in the three-hundred and eighteen during which you're trying to tell me the Regan became a champion of women's rights." She meant it too; she was interested. In addition to being the Regan, Darian was Markus's best friend. She respected Darian, but she also wanted to like him, as Markus did. If she was ever going to completely let go of the resentment she felt over being so closely controlled by him, something she genuinely wanted for everyone's sake, then she needed to understand him better. Knowing his past might help her forgive some of what she held against him in the present.

Sarah must have come to the same conclusion, because when she continued it was without anger. "Female rights. And whether you believe it or not, he's come leaps and bounds from where he began, never mind from his ancestors' positions—with a little help, of course." She stopped. She was smiling, a far off grin that made her look girlish, despite three-centuries of experience. "But that story took place long before he was Regan and has nothing to do with the Vengatti or why we're here."

"It sounds perfect." Alex leaned forward with her elbows on her knees.

Sarah shook her head. "There are certain parts I am sure Darian would not appreciate me repeating."

"You just told us how modern he was. Surely he wouldn't forbid you, as a free female, from telling us." Although it oozed with sarcasm, it was the first thing Ellie had said all night that wasn't also steeped in pain. Cormelia seemed to hear this and sympathized.

"Go on, Sarah. It'd be good for these young ones to hear what dating and mating used to be like."

Vivian eyed her roommate. "Are you including me as a 'young one'?"

"Anyone born in this country is still a babe to me, Vi."

Vivian rolled her eyes.

"Wait. If you were born here, than when did you and Sage meet?"

"Hush. You said you wanted a Vengatti-free tale. Sarah's the only one here with one of those."

Sarah had sat back down. She kicked off her silver flats and tucked her long lean legs under her. She closed her eyes briefly in defeat.

"I'm doing this against my better judgment as a favor to you two." She paused to point at both Alex and Ellie, who had turned around to face the circle. "If a word of this is breathed outside this room, I will not speak a single syllable to keep Darian from beating whoever's mate or partner it was. Understood?"

Alex and Ellie nodded then turned to one another. For a brief moment they exchanged a rare shared smile.

Lauren Grimley

2. Grace and Dignity:
Sarah & Darian's Story

Ireland, 1713

"Oh look, Mate, my birthday present has arrived a few weeks early."

Darian had entered the dark drive of his father's residence and sidled up to the carriage where Sarah was unloading her belongings. She had already sent her driver into the carriage house with the horses. Hearing his comment, which made her sound like a possession meant to please the prince, she didn't so much as look in his direction. She wouldn't be obligated to acknowledge him for what she hoped was at least another few months.

"Evening, Sarah." The poor young warrior who had been assigned as the future Regan's guard had trudged up behind him. His apologetic tone and the deep bow he greeted her with spoke volumes about how he felt towards his charge.

"Good evening, Markus," she said allowing him to kiss her hand. Though his father was the lead warrior and known for his brutality on the battlefield, Markus had been raised properly under the Regan's roof. That Darian had been raised alongside him, less than a decade younger, no one could have guessed.

"What am I, bog muck?" Darian asked as Markus released her hand.

"Not for much longer, I am told." Sarah pulled at the largest of her trunks. Markus immediately stepped forward to help her lift it from the back of the open-topped carriage. Darian didn't lift a finger except to rakishly adjust his cap over his long wavy hair like a fop.

"You'll miss abusing me once I'm matured, won't you?"

Markus snorted. Sarah met the young warrior's warm green eyes and smiled.

"Something amusing, warrior?" Darian demanded. Sarah wondered if he was angry at being laughed at or jealous of her and Markus's easy exchange, so contradictory to the tense, formal responses she usually provided him.

Markus didn't appear overly concerned with the cause of the future Regan's mood or his status as he continued to tease him. "Shocking, more like, that you could have grown up half a house away from me mom and da and actually believe that a female like Sarah will stop 'abusing' you, as you call it, simply because she's forced to mate you."

"Forced? Do you know how many females would give one of their fangs to be the Regan's mate?"

Sarah bit her tongue and let Markus reply for her.

"Yes, I had to spend the early evening hours clearing away the mob of them so Sarah's carriage could get to the gate." Markus easily eluded Darian's swing. The future Regan might have been quite a bit larger than the small warrior, but Markus had been matured for over seven years. Darian's speed and strength had been increasing tremendously over the last month, the very reason it had been determined that the time had come for Sarah to move into the Regan's home, but it wouldn't reach its peak until shortly after his maturity. Markus and Sarah both knew that when Darian's fangs came in their fun would end. He would be presented to the coven in an elaborate ceremony, which would only be outdone in extravagance by the mating ceremony that would soon follow. He would, from that day forth, demand the same respect the Regan or Elder Regan were given now—whether he deserved it or not.

"Bring her bags to her rooms before I have you beaten, you twat."

Markus's jaw dropped at the crude comment. "Darian, watch your language around her, or it'll be *you* your father's flaying. My apologies, Sarah, I'm not allowed to muzzle him—yet."

Sarah simply sighed. This was what her mother had spent nearly three decades training her for—to be the mate of a crass, precocious little boy. This was the great *honor* for which she had been chosen as an infant, years before the future Regan had even been born.

Darian brushed off the chastisement and watched smugly as Markus easily shouldered both the heavy trunks and headed to the house with them. When he was far enough down the drive that his dark silhouette blended in with the shadows, Darian turned to her. He swept off his hat and wrung it in his hands—nervously?

"Is he right? Do you feel forced?"

Now it was Sarah who wanted to swat at someone, but she figured even she couldn't get away with hitting the little prince. She hoped her exasperated tone of voice would get the message across.

"Why must you always do that?"

"Do what?"

"Put on a show for everyone. Do you think Markus is impressed by your lewd behavior? I've seen him with the female he fancies, Alia; he wouldn't dream of saying to her the things you say to me."

Sarah took the last small leather satchel in her hand, hiked up the heavy skirt of her long dress and headed up the gravelly path. Darian flashed in front of her, faster than he ought to have been able to.

"Just how close to maturity—"

"Answer my question, and then I'll answer yours."

"Both of them?"

Darian smiled. "Depends on how satisfactorily you answer mine."

Sarah lifted her chin. She looked past him into the dark damp fields surrounding the house. "Fine. I take the future of this coven seriously and know that my role in that is both an honor and a responsibility."

Darian groaned. "Spare me. Although I try hard to avoid them, I've sat in on enough Elder Council meetings to recognize diplomatic blarney when I hear it. That was a tactful way of avoiding the real question. Do you want to mate me or not?"

Sarah wanted to parlay with another insincere remark but that would be stooping to his level. The truth was she didn't know. In the few rare moments when Darian let down his guard and stopped trying to impress the warriors or irritate his father and the elders, there was something charming about him. Or maybe it was that in those moments she could still see the motherless little lad who once idolized her.

As a toddler, he'd follow her around on her annual

visits clinging to her skirts with his pudgy hand as soon as his father turned his back. When he was a bit older, he'd sneak into the kitchen with his wooden sword, like a warrior hunting Vengatti, in order to pilfer sweets for her. By then she was old enough to be expected to remain inside with the adults, to pour tea and look pretty during dry discussions of coven business. Darian did his best to entertain her by popping his head in windows or around doorways with his eyes crossed and his tongue wagging. It is impossible for vampire young to get away with such antics. He knew this, and he nearly always got caught and punished, but it never deterred him from trying again the next night. Being hopelessly naïve at that age, she had viewed this risky behavior for her benefit as early signs of chivalry.

She looked at the male before her now, still waiting impatiently for his answer. At over six feet, he no longer needed a wooden box to peek in the windows of the estate house behind him. His broad shoulders and muscled arms, coupled with the tan he had from sneaking out so many days, made him look more like a local farmhand or bog cutter than a future Regan, and far from the little babe she first met as her future mate. He certainly had changed in those intervening years. What she wasn't sure of was whether somewhere within he had retained any of the better traits for which she had once adored him.

"I've known you since you were in diapers—"

He threw his hands up. "That's not an answer, either."

"Then let me finish, please." She waited. He crossed his arms, but reluctantly agreed. "I've known you all that time, but I don't really know you, Darian. At least, I hope I don't. I hope you're not the obnoxious male you act like when the others are around, the one who, word has it, spends as much time in his father's stocks as the coven fool. I can't know if I want to mate you, until I know the real you."

"We have an official fool? How did I not know that?"

She shook her head. "I thought you wanted to be serious."

"Oh, I do." He looked her up and down while running his tongue over his lips. "Let's go." Darian reached out and grabbed her hand. He began leading her across the dewy field.

"Stop. Where are we going?" She gave a tug and easily broke his hold. He looked down at his empty hand. When he turned back to her, it was clear his mask was back in place.

"You said you wanted to *know* me before deciding whether you'd mate me. I'm happy to oblige, but not in my father's driveway. There's a very charming stand of trees at the far side of the property, though, that would suffice."

Sarah stepped back in shock. "You knew that wasn't my meaning. Who do you think I am, one of your human whores?"

He was laughing uncontrollably. "Come off it. I was jesting. Then again, if you did want a preview, to know what I've got to offer…" He heaved her body up against his, pressing himself against her in a way that made it more than clear what parts of him he was willing to let her preview.

She shoved hard at his chest, managing to break free from his vice tight grip. "You filthy swine. For your information, I helped your nurses bathe you plenty of times; I don't recall you having all that much to offer, to be honest."

Darian's faced burned from red to white. Sarah had seen Ardellus's coloring change the same, usually just prior to him beating someone to within an inch of his life. She didn't wait to see if his son had inherited the same violent reactions. She flashed to the house. At the front door she collided with someone exiting as she tried to enter. She teetered in the new, heeled boots in which her mother had sent her off.

"Sarah, are you okay? Did he…are you hurt?"

It was only Markus. *Thank the Creator.* It was clear from the way his eyes looked her up and down that he was wondering what had caused the ruckus she and Darian had just been making.

"I'm fine. Unless the whole house just heard that." The heat in her cheeks flared as he responded.

"I think the better part of County Cork heard that. Serves him right, too," Markus whispered the final words. Sarah looked past him into the house.

"How much trouble will I be in for addressing him so?"

"You?" Markus chortled. "The Regan's been watching and listening from his office window. He didn't send me out to drag you in by your hair."

"Now, warrior." The disembodied bark came from the second floor causing Markus to jump.

"Yes, Regan."

As Markus stepped around her, she caught his sleeve. "Hurry, he's much faster than he ought to be for someone as far from his maturity as I was told he is."

Markus nodded. "I know. Don't believe everything you hear." He was whispering again. "His incisors have been aching him for weeks. He hasn't told his father because he knows his maturity will mean a tighter leash. And it's about time, too."

There was another flash. Sarah startled. She cringed on Markus's behalf when she realized it was his father, the elder Markus, who was the coven's lead warrior.

"Did you not hear the Regan? Go get him. If he's not lashed to that tree out back and beaten before sunrise, guess who'll be beside him tomorrow night?"

Markus threw his hands up in protest. "Da, he's halfway to Dublin by now."

The elder grabbed his son's ear like he was still a boy. "Then why are you still here gabbing with the females? Go." He shoved Markus out into the waning night and turned to bow deeply to Sarah. Without a word he was gone, replaced by another.

In his usual way, the Regan managed to set her on edge with just his posture, too erect, too forbidding to be welcoming, despite his words.

"Lady Sarah, welcome to your new home." Ardellus took her hand and kissed it lightly. "I hope my son hasn't already soured you to it. I assure you, he will be dealt with, severely."

"No."

Ardellus dropped her hand in surprise.

The word, which few ever spoke to a Regan, had slipped from her lips, and like someone fumbling etched crystal over stone flags, grasping for it was useless. Still, she tried to explain.

"Please, Regan, his comments and actions were crass, but so was my response to them. I would appreciate it if we could forget the whole incident ever happened."

"I don't overlook mistreatment of females. As part of your duties will soon be to represent them, you shouldn't either. He will apologize and then be punished. As for you, I think considering the position he put you in, especially after a tiring trip, an apology is sufficient."

"Of course, Regan. I'm so sorry that I—"

"Not to me, Sarah. To Darian."

"Oh." Sarah had to look at her feet to keep her shock and anger from being evident. "Yes, Regan."

He lifted her chin with a finger. "Your respect is clearly something he'll need to earn. And I'll do my best to see he learns the proper way to do that. But your deference, as with the rest of the coven's, will soon be required. Mate or not, you will always be a female, and he will always be a Regan—future, current, or elder. Understood?"

"Yes, Regan." Sarah bowed her spine obediently, feeling every bone and muscle strain to maintain the dignity and grace her father had instilled in her, while relinquishing every last bit of independence. She reminded herself of the words she had spoken to Darian, the same words her mother ingrained in her nightly growing up: this was an honor.

Late the next afternoon Sarah sat on a stool by her bedroom window drinking in the sun that filtered through the milky clouds. She wasn't able to sleep, yet in her quiet trance memories came to her like dreams.

She was ten, crouched beneath her father's desk crying, hiding to escape more of her mother's sharp criticisms. Her father had been home from the Elder Council meeting, which was held in a back room of the village pub, less than a minute before discovering her there.

"Sarah, is that you?"

A sob shook her as she braced herself for further scolding.

"What's the matter, little one?" His soft features as he bent over to address her gave her the courage she needed to answer.

"Mother says, even with nearly a decade's head start, I'll never be good enough."

"She said precisely that?"

Sarah pouted. Her father always knew when she was telling tales. "She meant that. And what she said was just as cruel."

"Oh?"

"She said the sheep could learn Latin quicker than I am."

Her father laughed. "Did it occur to you, little lamb, that she was only teasing you? That it was meant to be a jest?"

She sniffed noisily. "Someone ought to tell her that she's not terribly funny."

"Excuse me?"

"Nothing, sir."

"Come out from under there."

Her pink lip trembled as she crawled out from under the heavy wooden desk and stood before him, eyes downcast. She had gone too far. He'd punish her now for sure.

Instead he merely lifted her chin. "That someone ought to be you."

She looked at him dumbfounded.

"People will treat you how you let them, Sarah. Your mother pushes you hard because she wants the best for you, but if you feel it's too much, you need to push back, politely, but firmly. You've been promised to the most powerful male in the coven—the future Regan. I can assure you that the Regan, his father, will see to it he is strong, of body and mind. You'll need to match his strength if you're to be his protector."

"But won't I make everyone angry if I say whatever I

think?"

Her father sat in the desk chair so that he was eye-level with her. "Very. So don't say whatever you think. Say what you know to be true. Say it honestly with grace and dignity. Most can handle even unpleasant truths when presented in the right way, by the right one."

"Am I the right one?" It was the question Sarah had asked herself with every new mistake, every criticism, since she was old enough to understand what her future role would be.

"When your time comes, I think you will be." He gave her blond braid a tug. "But let's see. Pretend I'm your mother and I've just compared your pronunciation to that of the pigs. What would you say to me?"

"I'd say that if the farm animals make such good students, then perhaps you ought to instruct them."

Her father crossed his arms over his barrel chest. "I'd say that would get you sent to bed with a very sore bottom. Try again."

"Yes, sir."

Sarah squinted as she thought. Dignity and grace had been ingrained in her since she was a tot. She knew exactly how to play those roles when she met the Regan or sat through long dinners with other first families. But honesty, of the kind her father spoke, had always been reserved for the private conversations the two shared, because it often seemed to conflict with her mother's rules of etiquette and respect. Her father wanted her to mesh them.

Sarah made another attempt. "I'd admit that my pronunciation isn't perfect yet, but remind her that until I've worked to make it so, it isn't polite to criticize the poor pigs."

She watched her father's expression, holding back her

own smile until she saw his lips twitch beneath his beard.

"Better. When you manage to balance that boldness with sincerity, you'll be the right one, not only the right female for the future Regan, but the right female to help guide the coven."

Sarah's father had said this as if she would help lead, help steer Darian to do the right things, to make the right decisions. He had raised her to be her mate's protector, but also his confidant and his advisor.

Ardellus had made it clear upon her arrival that both she and her father had been mistaken. She was not entering into a relationship; she was filling a role. Therefore, she was to take orders, like any other coven member. The strength she'd developed over the twenty years since would be put to only one use: to help her obey night after night without losing hold entirely of her dignity.

Sarah lifted her head, almost feeling her father's cool touch under her chin, and swallowed to ease the lump in her throat. She quickly dressed and found her way back through the large house to the front entryway. Her fingers were on the handle of the ornately carved wooden door, which she had entered so shaken the night before, when a male appeared at her side. She let escape a cry. As a first family, her own parents' house was nearly as large and well-protected as the Regan's, but the sudden appearance of this husky, armed warrior had startled her. The way he now positioned himself between her and the door, however, frustrated her.

"Hush. You'll wake the Regan. Why are you out of bed?" he asked, as if the answer were his business.

"I couldn't sleep, so I dressed. I'm accustomed to taking a walk in the early evening." Sarah started for the door handle again.

He impeded her path, but rather than appearing threatening, his expression softened. "I'm afraid you'll need to get unaccustomed to that—at least until your mate stops disappearing during the days. Markus is the only fully-trained warrior living in the house who can still go out in the sun, and he spends half his time sticking his head in nearby barns where Darian's known to romp with his human play-things."

"Nicolo!"

Sarah spun at the sound of an admonishing female voice. Markus's mother Diane stood at the other end of the foyer, hands on her hips. An untied apron hung from her neck. It was clear she had been preparing to start the Regan's breakfast when she overheard the warrior's crass comment.

"It's fine, Diane. I understand that not all of the warriors were raised properly like your Markus. And for your information, Nicolo, I've managed my nightly walks without a warrior since the days when the only romping Darian was doing was done in his diapers." She reached again for the door, but this time Nicolo grabbed her wrist.

"Perhaps, Lady Sarah, but you've never before been less than a year from mating our future Regan, while wanting to wander the property known by the Vengatti to belong to the current Regan. Though the warriors won't officially pledge ourselves to you until your mating ceremony, it is still our duty to protect you. Right now that means keeping you in the house." Nicolo released her wrist. His fist went to his heart as he bowed. It was the warrior's pledge, a gesture she'd only ever seen used between warriors or given to the Regan.

Sarah took a step back. This was a shock of a

different kind. She wondered how many more she'd face in the days ahead in this new life.

Diane seemed to see her struggle and came to her side. "Thank you, Nicolo. I think Sarah understands, but watch your tongue next time when addressing her, or my son and Darian won't be the only two on the receiving end of my mate's fury."

"Yes, ma'am." Nicolo shrunk like it was his own mother scolding him. Sarah supposed in many ways it was. As mate to the lead warrior, whom many would argue was second in command, and the female in charge of the Regan's household, Diane made many of these males' meals, stitched their wounds, and, when tragedy struck, sometimes even prepared their ashes for their returning ceremonies. She was an honorary mother to them all. Her strength and her compassion had earned their respect. Sarah made note of it as she contemplated her new role.

"Sarah, since you're up, how about helping me in the kitchen?"

A blush crept up Sarah's cheeks. Diane seemed to see it.

"Not that you need to. As Darian's partner you'll never be required to do such things, but I thought you might like something to keep you busy, and perhaps some female company."

"Oh, no. Please don't mistake me." Sarah didn't think such work beneath her. She was well aware that most females in the coven worked sunset to sunrise to care for their families, something neither she nor her mother had ever had to do. She had tremendous respect for such work. It was just—

"I don't know how. To cook, I mean."

Diane chuckled. "I suspected as much, which is partly

why I asked. It's my belief that every female ought to know how to keep her own house. There may be a time when you and the young Regan will want a little more independence. The fewer people you need to rely on, the freer you'll both be to find your own way." Diane paused to look around at the many doors and hallways off the large foyer. Sarah wondered how many people the Regan relied on to maintain it all. "It's your choice, though."

Choice and independence. Diane was offering her two things which mere moments ago she had feared she'd rarely have again.

"I'd love to learn, and I appreciate you teaching me more than you can imagine."

Diane smiled in a way that left Sarah wondering if maybe she could imagine. "Then follow me, girl."

An hour later Sarah helped Diane carry the breakfast dishes into the main dining room where the Regan was already sitting with a pile of papers and a pot of tea before him.

"Thank you, Di…Sarah?" He looked first to her then to Diane for explanation, something he seemed to expect immediately and without having to ask for it. Diane appeased him in her own way.

"I'm just seeing to it that the excellent education and training her mother began is completed before their mating day, Regan."

"There's no need for it." Ardellus put down the paper he'd been holding and held Diane's gaze. If he expected an obedient nod, he was disappointed in her response.

"Sarah is not here merely to fulfill the needs of the coven, nor of your son. Not tonight, certainly, but some night perhaps, she will want to do something to please him. A fine meal has always pleased you." Diane gently ran her hand down the Regan's upper arm. His scowl seemed to soften. Sarah suspected it took years of trust to exact such a response. Still, she knew she'd do well to remember it. "The lamb stew you request with such frequency was Daphne's recipe, not mine, if I recall."

Ardellus stiffened at the mention of his deceased mate. Then he looked at the empty chair across from him.

"For breakfast and occasionally dinner, then. She'll have other tasks to attend to some nights." He looked up again at each of them.

"Yes, Regan," they replied. Diane winked at her before disappearing into the kitchen. The dishes all served, Sarah sat down to eat in silence as the Regan returned to his papers and his plate. Eventually he sighed and put down the letter he was reading. With one more glance at the seat that had remained empty since Darian's birth nearly twenty years before, he faced her.

"You will want to please him someday, just as he'll want to please you. And I suspect the credit for both of those will lay with you. I have taught him the lessons he needs to one day be a decent Regan. It was Daphne's role to teach him how to be a decent male and mate. I never managed to fill the hole left by her returning. That falls to you now, I suppose." He paused to scrutinize her. She felt as if he could see her very essence; she wanted badly to look away. She didn't. He nodded, in what might have been approval. "Your father has assured me for years that you have both the strength and the compassion to do what needs to be done for my son, for the coven. I hope he is right." Ardellus didn't wait for a response from the stunned Sarah before returning to his work. "You may be excused," he said without looking back at her.

Sarah stood and left the room with her head spinning.

Breathing in the dewy night air, Sarah knew she had

been right to insist on this one source of serenity. She had been summoned after lunch to the Regan's office where he sat in front of an aromatic peat fire with the elder Markus. She had assumed they had found Darian and she was being called in to make her apology before he was punished in the brutal way his father still employed to keep the coven and his son under control. Looking around the office she had soon realized she was mistaken. Darian was still missing, though neither the Regan nor the lead warrior seemed overly concerned about him. They had gathered instead to discuss her security. Once again, Sarah was disconcerted by the seriousness that was shown for her safety. She was appreciative, moved even, but knew that for the preservation of her sanity, she'd have to put her foot down, gently, but firmly, as her father would have said.

The elder Markus had finally consented to an after dinner walk, so long as she promised precaution. She was to stay on the heavily guarded grounds and return a half hour before the first hint of light on the eastern horizon. Upon her return she would report to the warrior on duty at the house before retiring.

"If any one of these requirements is not met on any night, the privilege will be revoked, Sarah. Is that clear?" Ardellus had demanded her assurance.

"Yes, Regan. And thank you, Markus," she had answered before being dismissed.

After the previous twenty-four hours, she would have promised anything for this short stretch of solitude. She could have ambled for hours along the fields without ever having left coven property. Like many land owners in Ireland, Ardellus and many of the first families had acquired tremendous amounts of acreage, then let out the fields to tenants to farm and herd. Not only did this allow them and the coven members, who were their tenants, to blend in, it also surrounded their homes with a buffer zone of other Rectinatti. Despite the relative safety this provided, Sarah was quite sure the elder Markus and the Regan had intended for her to stay on the property proper. At a stand of trees, which seemed to mark the edge of land used by the Regan, she began to turn back.

As she rounded the corner there was a rustling behind her, followed by a quiet clunk. Sarah spun, her hand digging into the pocket of her dress. A figure had appeared behind her and lunged for her wrist. She jerked out the small dirk her father had insisted she carry and slashed the arm of her attacker.

Darian watched as the bloodstain began to blossom on the sleeve of his dirty linen shirt.

"You knew it was me."

It wasn't a question, and Sarah didn't deny it. She stood defiant.

He looked up, eyes flashing—fangs fully elongated. Darian had reached full maturity. She had just spilled the blood of a Regan.

"Coven members have been burned as traitors for less than that." His voice was a growl.

Her hand shook, but she didn't drop the short blade.

"Apologize now. On your knees." Darian reached for her again, pushing down hard on her shoulder. He intended to make her grovel for forgiveness, something that was well within his rights now that he was a full-fanged vampire and son of a Regan. How quickly he had slipped into the role of ruler.

Ardellus's words from breakfast rang in her head. He wanted her to teach him to be a decent male and mate, but how could she do that groveling before him?

"No."

Reacting much the way his father had to the infrequently heard syllable, Darian jerked back as if he'd been struck. Unlike the last time she spoke the word, she had no desire to take it back.

"First, you don't deserve an apology." She wrenched her shoulder from his grasp.

"And secondly?"

Sarah couldn't be sure, but she thought an undertone of amusement had seeped into Darian's voice.

"Because you'd never respect me again if I did. I wouldn't deserve your respect if I did." The words began spilling out. They were the truth, a truth Darian needed to hear from her. "Your father, the Regan, has little tolerance and even less respect for those who grovel at his feet, especially when it's clear they disagree with him. I suspect he's taught you to feel much the same way. It is the reason I'm here. My father is one of the few elders who has never shied away from speaking his mind in the Regan's presence, even to share his dissent. If your father hadn't been convinced I could be taught to do the same, I never would have been chosen to be your mate at such an early age. I will bow to you when the eyes of the coven are watching, when it is the right example to set. But if you enter into a mating with me and expect me to protect you and sustain you with my essence, than you better do it as my equal, or I assure you, feeding from me will provide you with nothing more than a mouthful of bitter-tasting blood."

Darian's expression was unreadable at first. With his fangs still sprung, she half expected him to lunge for her throat, to force from her the essence she claimed she'd deny him. The knife was still in her hand, but she let it drop to her side as she squared her shoulders. It was this final act that evoked a response. Not the one she had expected.

He laughed.

"Well done. For once my father made the right choice for me." His fangs snapped back in. He reached a finger to his mouth and sprung them again, like a child playing with a new toy. Discovering her watching him, he retracted them and dropped his hand.

Sarah's stuttering boiled over into rage. "This was all a test? The way you've treated me the last two nights? The things you've said to me? Grabbing me from behind? You pompous, deceitful little—" She stopped and drew in a deep breath. What was it about him that caused her to forget herself, her dignity, time and time again?

"Don't stop on my account," Darian teased, leaning against a tree with an air that made her want to punch him. It was clear he wanted her to disgrace herself further by continuing. Her job, however, was not to give him what he wanted, but rather what he and the coven needed. She collected herself, shook her head, and returned her knife to the pocket of her dress. He fumbled for a response after realizing she planned to remain silent.

"Look, you said yourself that you didn't want to mate someone you didn't know. Why should I be any different? Actually, the difference is that I have a choice. My father wouldn't be pleased if I refused to mate you, but now that I'm matured, he couldn't force me. Luckily, it won't come to that."

It was Sarah's turn to sputter. "Because I've lost my temper on you twice? First insulting your...pride. Next nearly taking off your arm. I hate to disappoint you, but those reactions are far from how I normally behave."

Darian groaned. "I've seen how you 'normally' behave on your yearly visits or at the ball. I know you can dance, and curtsy, and charm the elders. So can half the other females in the coven. Not many can deliver a biting comeback or wield a knife against a Regan, and those who can are likely crass, uneducated, and ill bred. Or they have a death wish. That's not why you've done them, I hope? You aren't so desperate at the thought of having to mate me that you're hoping my father will execute you instead? If so, you'll be sorely disappointed; he prefers slow, painful punishments, unfortunately." Darian rubbed his backside and cringed for her benefit.

Sarah knew he was teasing, but answered despite herself.

"Prior to last night, I was withholding judgment until I got to know you, the real you."

Darian's expression grew more serious. He ran his hands through his hair. He had apparently lost the foolish woolen cap during his flight the previous night. "And now?"

Sarah sighed. She walked to another tree among the copse and sat on the mossy ground beneath it, tucking her feet up under her skirts.

"I'm confused."

"Well, that's better than repulsed." He moved closer to her, a grin playing on his lips. He stopped short of sitting beside her. Instead he rested his arm on the tree she sat against as he asked her to explain.

"I ought to despise you. In the one night I've been here you have purposely frightened me, insulted me, and threatened me, all to see whether I measured up to your daft standards."

"Yet you don't despise me." It was a statement, said with cocky assurance, another reason she ought not to have continued. Once again, though, the truth was hard to contain.

"No. How can I when I have similar standards? Even

a female whose mating's been arranged most of her life still thinks about what she wants in a mate. I've always wanted a male who is strong and cunning and who respects me for being the same." Darian's grin was growing. Sarah set him straight. "But I also want a mate who is honest and compassionate. From what I gather, you're honest with no one, save perhaps with your best mate Markus, and you certainly don't show him any compassion. Do you know the trouble he's in because of you? He spent all night and day searching for you knowing that his father intended to beat the both of you, even if he did manage to find you."

Darian scoffed and slid his back down the trunk of the tree opposite her.

"I assure you that Markus quit searching for me within minutes of starting. He likely spent a very pleasant day with his fangs in his female, which will more than make up for whatever punishment he gets later."

"After the rumors I've heard about you, Darian, you should be the last one saying such things about Markus and Alia." She pretended to be insulted on the other couple's behalf, but she was also curious. Nicolo's comment earlier that evening hadn't been the first she had heard about Darian's promiscuous behavior.

He smirked, guessing correctly which part of her comment weighed more heavily on her. "Rumors about how I've bedded every loose-kneed Irish farm girl from here to Dublin, supposedly in their human fathers' barns in broad daylight? None of that sounded like blarney to you?"

Sarah felt her cheeks redden. "I tried not to dwell on the logistics of your indiscretions. The point is, though rumors grow like weeds, they often begin with a seed of truth."

"Unless they're planted by the one they're about."

Sarah sat up and straightened her skirts. "You mean to say that *you* started them?"

"With Markus's help." Darian's warm brown eyes gleamed, daring her to call his bluff. She fell for it.

"I don't believe you. The young Markus's reputation is as impeccable as his father's."

Darian nodded, but his smug grin faded quickly. "Yes, and because of all of my other indiscretions, which Markus does keep quiet about, I felt I owed it to him to cover for him after a nosey coven member heard him and Alia in a nearby stable one evening. I made sure I had a few extra pints the next night, sitting beside a table of warriors, as I bragged to Markus of my roll in the hay with a human from the village. Sure enough, it spread and grew from there. And I couldn't be happier."

"But why?" Sarah leaned forward to try to read his expression. When he saw her watching him, Darian began to dig in the dirt with the blade from one of the knives he wore on his belt.

"Countless reasons. First, it's my fault Markus has to hide his relationship with Alia. His father won't let him mate until I'm 'settled down,' for fear that his own family concerns would distract him from keeping a close enough eye on me. A concern he wouldn't have if I hadn't been slipping my guard and wandering the county during the days since I was ten." Grasping the handle of the knife, Darian drew it over his shoulder and released it. Sarah's eyes followed its projection and watched it split the bark of a sapling. "That's the second reason." He grinned, satisfied with his aim and his newfound strength. "In exchange for my giving him what he most desires a few days a month, he gives me what I want most: a chance at the Vengatti."

She gasped. "But you've just matured. That's terribly dangerous. No, as the only heir, it's foolish *and* selfish."

Darian rolled his eyes. "You sound like my father. And Markus, for that matter. He hasn't actually allowed me to hunt them. He's just been training me to track and to fight." Darian's eyes gleamed. "Though now I'm matured, he'll have to take me on real patrols. All Regans have served as warriors before ascending."

Sarah shook her head. There was no use telling him she disagreed with this tradition.

"Your reputation seems a heavy price to pay for a few wrestling lessons."

Darian picked at the moss at his feet. "But not too much for Markus. He's the closest thing I have to a friend. And leading can be lonely. Just look at my father." The second half of his statement was as quiet as a breath, but Sarah heard it. It was the first time she detected any vulnerability, any tenderness to Darian's words.

She appreciated his honesty. She reached forward to give his arm a gentle squeeze. "It doesn't have to be."

His wince startled her. Then she remembered the earlier injury she had caused him.

"I'm sorry. I forgot."

He brushed aside her apology. "It's a scratch." He turned his wrist and pulled back his sleeve to prove his point, but what he revealed was more of a gash. Her light touch had started it bleeding anew.

"Here. Let me stop the bleeding." Sarah moved closer to his side and reached for his hand. Kneeling by his right leg she brought his arm to her mouth and began to lick clean the cut, using her venom to heal the wound.

As his blood touched her tongue, something sparked. Her fangs sprang as the sweetness slid down her throat. She had been sustained on her mother and father's essence since her maturity almost a decade ago. Never before had feeding felt like this. Her body reacted in ways she was sure were forbidden before her mating night, yet there was no repressing the warmth or tingling that left parts of her aching. She realized she had been deeply drawing in Darian's essence when he let escape a moan. Flicking her tongue over the rest of the gash, she let his arm drop.

"No, it's okay. I just...I haven't fed since I matured."

"Earlier tonight?" She realized she hadn't gotten around to asking him before.

"Some time during the day. I woke up...thirsty and realized my fangs had come in."

Sarah saw the glistening on his elongated fangs. It was the venom vampires excreted during feeding. Most young vampires fed immediately upon maturing; their bodies build a need for essence in the months prior. He had to be starving for it. If the intensity of their conversation hadn't kept her senses otherwise occupied, she would have smelled it sooner.

With his essence on her lips, she could taste the assurance she had sought, that under the brutish façade was a decent male. She hardly hesitated before offering.

"Do you know how?" She was already out of her jacket and was untucking her blouse from her skirts.

"I think I can figure it out." Darian's eyes lit up as he went for his belt. Sarah slapped his hand away. She ignored the bulging below it.

"I meant to feed, to draw essence."

"But—" He watched her undressing in confusion.

"I'm removing my blouse because it's not always possible to be neat your first few times."

She watched him staring at her as she lay back on the springy moss wearing only her tightly laced bodice.

Twisting her long blond hair behind her head, she wondered if his pained look was caused by the desire she was about to satisfy or by the one she had just denied. When he suddenly straddled her, lowering his body gently onto hers so his mouth brushed her exposed neck, she was quite sure it was a bit of each.

She expected him to hesitate; she gasped when he bit into her flesh with no delay.

Darian pulled out immediately.

"Did I hurt you? Did I do something wrong?" His eyes darted from her neck to her face. They were filled with genuine concern. The realization made her heart flutter again like it had when she fed from him. Her response was breathy.

"No. I mean, it always hurts a bit, but you're doing fine, except for letting my blood run down my neck."

"Right." Darian twirled his tongue around her neck to lick up what had escaped his two fang marks. With his first swallow he pushed himself up once again. This time his eyes searched hers so completely that she was sure her essence had had the same effect on him that his had had on her.

"If this is bitter," he referenced her earlier threat, "I'm not sure I ever want to taste sweet." He was licking his lips grotesquely.

Sarah groaned. "Spare me the flowery praise and drink, will you?"

Darian winked and returned to drink heavily from her vein. He pulled too hard and took too much. She'd be bruised and weak tomorrow night, but she didn't stop him. Finally, he ran his tongue over the wounds. The essence exchange complete, propriety ought to have sent him away. Instead his nose pushed into her hair, then nudged along her jawbone. His long waves curtained their faces like a modesty veil, though she felt anything but modest as a strand brushed her cheeks and sent a ripple down her entire body. Suddenly his lips were on hers, full and forceful. She turned her head to the side to stop him. When he reached with his callused fingers to turn her towards him, though, she found her lips parting to allow his tongue to touch her own. She could taste her own blood, her own essence, while still feeling the effects of Darian's. She gave into the kisses, even nipping at his bottom lip when he pulled back.

When she felt his hand grasp once again at his belt buckle, she pushed him off.

"Darian, stop. This isn't right."

"Why not?" he asked returning his lips to hers, making a response nearly impossible.

"We're not mated," she managed between his continued advances.

"We will be soon." One hand was tugging at the laces of her bodice.

"We hardly know each other," she said entwining her fingers in his to keep him from reaching his goal.

He finally stopped and looked at her. "How can you say that with my essence inside you? Do you think there's anyone right now who knows me better? Who knows you better? I know enough to know I want you."

Sarah shook her head. She didn't disagree with what he said. She just wasn't sure of the reasons he said it.

"You've just fed for the first time. Your senses are heightened, as are your desires. You don't know what you want, because you want everything. A plate of lamb stew would likely leave you hard at the moment."

Darian's eyes widened at her boldness, but seeing the blush in her cheeks, he grew bolder himself. With the hand holding hers, he pinned one arm above her head, then the other. His other hand freed her breast from her fitted undergarment, his fingers running over her hardened nipple.

"And what's your excuse?"

There was no denying her body wanted what his did. That wasn't the problem.

"You said you wanted us to be honest with one another. Can you honestly tell me you don't want this?"

Her eyes squeezed shut as she breathed out an answer, "Not for the same reason you do."

Darian sat up releasing her hands. "What the hell does that mean?"

With a quick shove she managed to slip out from under him. She sat facing away hugging her knees.

"Sarah." He had flashed around in front of her. He wasn't angry. He looked confused. And when he saw what she tried to hide from him, he looked scared, a bit like the child he had left behind permanently with his first mouthful of her essence. "Are you...crying? Oh, Creator. Please tell me you know I'd never force you. Last night was a joke. And tonight—I thought you wanted to." His voice trailed off. Sarah heard the hurt in it.

"I did. I do."

Darian sat back on his heels. "Markus was right. You females are a puzzling lot."

Sarah smiled even as a sob shook her. "I won't apologize for my gender, but I will apologize for me."

"No apologizing, not after all I've done." He reached out a grubby thumb to smear the remaining tears from her pale cheeks. "Just explain, please."

She nodded. "You want me because your feeding has aroused you, but I want you because your essence has convinced me..."

"Of what?"

"That I'll fall in love with you."

Darian crossed his arms over his chest and tensed his square jaw. "Though we detest gushing about them, your kind does not have a monopoly on emotions. For future reference, you've aroused me since I was eleven and you greeted me with a hug, allowing my face to feel a female's breast for the first time—"

"Ew, that's incredibly crass."

"But honest." He shrugged. "As for falling for you, that happened sometime between when you quite loudly questioned my malehood and when you sliced open my arm. Tasting your essence sealed the deal. Making love to you was going to be the icing on the already delicious cake." Darian stood up. "But if you haven't fallen for me yet, then I guess you're right. We should wait." He turned his back and made to walk away, though his discomfort was obvious from his stiff gait.

It was her turn to flash in front of him. With one good shove, she had him on his back. He might have been a six and a half foot male, but he was newly matured. She had nine years on his strength. Her hands unlaced her bodice and flung it aside, baring her breasts in the veiled moonlight. She squeezed his chin so he met her eyes, though his desperately wanted to be looking a bit south.

"If you tell anyone, Markus included, I'll swear you forced yourself upon me and watch with pleasure as your father strips all but an inch of skin from your back. Understood?"

Darian could do no more than nod. Satisfied, Sarah stripped his pants past his knees with a rough tug. Freed from the restraints of the fabric, it was clear her insults the previous night were unfounded.

He took advantage of her shock and in one swift

movement reversed their positions. He pulled her skirts up and with a wicked grin leaned over to whisper in her ear.

"I've grown a wee bit over the years." With no further preamble he pushed himself inside her. It took all her restraint not to cry out at his first thrust. Soon, though, she found, like with feeding, that the pleasure far outstripped the pain. There'd be decades for slow explorative lovemaking. Tonight, neither had the patience. She wrapped her long legs around his waist and dug her nails deeper into his shoulders with each push. Their eyes locked as he rocked his hips against hers, rubbing her nipples with his rough thumbs. The gleam she saw wasn't one of conquest, a look she would have expected from the masked Darian. This was the look of one who'd just discovered the one other vampire from whom he'd never have to hide again.

When her body began to shudder and Darian could no longer hold back, they both cried out. Sarah could feel the new exchange of fluids happening inside her, as warm and potent as their essence exchange. When it ceased, Darian froze for a moment, still deep between her thighs. They were both listening for the sound of footfalls, Markus's or another warrior's, bounding across the field after them. When none came, they shared a relieved smile. Darian slid out from her and collapsed beside her, looking as exhausted as she felt. With his head on her shoulder, she lay listening to his breathing growing slower and shallower with her own.

The sunlight on her face warmed her. It was so rare in Ireland to have sun as strong as this. She wanted to relish in it. When she went to stretch out her arm, something, or someone, was on it.

Her eyes flashed open as she sprung to her feet. Darian's head hit the damp ground with a soft thud.

"What are you doing?" He blinked against the brightness as he rubbed the spot on his head that had hit the dirt.

"Get up. Get dressed. It's midmorning already."

"Exactly. So why are we getting up?"

In her panic, Sarah struggled with the ties on her blouse. "I was supposed to check in a half hour before sunrise. I promised your father and the elder Markus. They'll be worried. Or furious."

"They'll be asleep, which is where we ought to be. Unless you're up for other daytime activities?" Darian was now awake. All parts of him were awake. Sarah turned away blushing, her modesty having returned in the daylight.

"Put your pants on. We need to find Markus and go back to the house."

"Together? With my fang print on your neck? That's your plan?"

She could hear him dressing, but didn't turn around. "Yes. Finding you nearly dying of thirst after your maturation and staying to feed you might partially excuse my egregious mistake of not returning when I promised I would."

He flashed before her. "Is Miss Honesty going to fib to the Regan and his lead warrior?"

"No, you are. You have much more practice than I do. I'll get us both killed for sure." Sarah wrung her skirts in her hand, a nervous habit she had since she was a girl.

"I assure you it's only him, and maybe me, they want to kill," an amused voice came from above.

Sarah's hand clutched her chest as Markus dropped almost silently from a branch fifteen feet above their

47

heads. Darian chuckled as he tucked in the back of his shirt, but Sarah stammered.

"How long…" She couldn't even look at him any more.

Markus seemed to sense her discomfort and answered reassuringly and without inquiry. "Only since sunrise." When he turned to Darian his voice took on a terser tone. "I followed your scent from our hiding spot. You didn't even try to mask it like I've taught you. If I'd been a Vengatti, you'd be dead and your partner…" He let the rest go unspoken.

Sarah noticed she was pleased Markus had described her as Darian's partner.

"If you were a Vengatti, I would have smelled you a half mile out, but let's pretend I thought you were." Before Markus or Sarah could ask what he meant, Darian swung at him. His fist glanced off Markus's chin before the more experienced warrior could dodge and withdraw his knife.

"What's wrong with you?"

Darian smiled widely, showing off his new fangs to remind Markus he had fully matured. The warrior begrudgingly stowed away his weapon.

"I suspect that's what your father will ask you when he sees you've injured me." Darian held out his bloody sleeve.

"I didn't—" Markus stopped. He looked at Sarah.

"You don't have to take the blame. I'll tell them—"

Markus held up his hand. "It's fine, Sarah. I'll play along, for you." He spun on Darian. "You on the other hand, owe me, fangs or no fangs."

Darian shrugged as he took Sarah's arm in his and headed to the house. She turned to try to thank the young warrior, but he brushed it off as if he were far too used to such treatment. She marveled at how deeply Markus must have loved both his female and his friend.

When they reached the front door it was locked. Darian and Markus exchanged a glance which told Sarah this wasn't what either expected or hoped for. Markus sucked in a deep breath and raised his fist to knock. Darian stopped him.

"Wait." He turned to Sarah and kissed first her left cheek, then her right. When he leaned in to kiss her lips, she pulled back.

"Darian." She looked meaningfully at Markus. Such public displays would hardly be sanctioned even after their mating.

"Sorry, but I have a feeling I won't be let out of his sight long enough to do that for awhile."

Sarah looked around. "Markus's?"

"Mine." With a click the door swung open. Scarcely beyond the threshold of sunlight stood the Regan.

Though he had already grown taller than his father and would outstrip his strength and size in a few short years, she was sure she saw Darian tremble at Ardellus's expression. It was nothing compared to how her own knees shook as she took in his brutal scowl and the thick braided bullwhip wrapped around his right hand.

It was only Markus who kept his cool. He grasped her elbow and led her inside. He didn't so much as glance at his own father who stood just inside the door. Approaching the Regan, he bowed deeply and begged his pardon.

"Sarah's weak after having to feed the young Regan. Might I escort her to her room so she could lie down while Darian explains?"

Ardellus's gaze scoured each of them, lingering on Markus's bruised jaw, Darian's bloody sleeve, and finally landing on Sarah's neckline. She was sure her blouse wasn't high enough to cover the marks Darian had left.

He looked back at the young warrior and nodded. "We'll be in the cellar when you've seen her settled in."

Markus hadn't made it two steps holding her arm when his father called to him.

"Don't dawdle. We'll be waiting for you, too."

"Yes, Da, ah, Sir." With that he swept Sarah down the nearest hallway.

Sarah was never quite sure whether she had fainted or simply fallen into a sudden and deep sleep the moment Markus had left her, but her next recollection was of being roused by one of Diane's assistants who was telling her to wash and dress for dinner. She had slept all through the day and well into the next night.

It was with a slight sense of dread that she entered the dining room, tugging the high lace collar of her blouse to hide the bruises that had burgeoned in her sleep. Adding to that, she once again found herself alone with Ardellus. She wondered how she'd make it through another meal as she curtsied and greeted him. Before she even unfolded her linen napkin, though, Darian was in the doorway. His bearing was stiff as he headed to his seat across from her. She saw his jaw tense as he sat gingerly in the straight-back wooden chair. He was trying to hide his pain from his father who watched keenly.

"Evening, father," he greeted curtly.

"Evening, Darian. I see you got my message," Ardellus paused. Sarah was quite sure any son, matured or not, would have been able to decipher the unspoken message evident in his countenance. Yet Darian remained mute. "My request you attend dinner," Ardellus clarified. "Are your gums still sore?"

Unable to ignore a direct question, Darian replied through gritted teeth. "My *gums* feel much better now that my fangs have come in, thank you."

When he turned to Sarah, his countenance softened. "Dia dhuit, Sarah." It was an Irish greeting, one the vampires adopted and used with reverence for their Creator and toward the one to whom it was spoken.

Sarah's cheeks flushed. "Dia is Muire dhuit, Darian," she replied quietly. She could feel Ardellus's eyes on her and was relieved when Diane entered with the dinner tray.

"Nice of you to join us tonight, Darian," she said sounding almost sincere as she placed the first bowl down in front of the Regan. "I've made you and your father's favorite tonight in honor of last night's event." Diane placed the second bowl in front of him and gave his back a hearty pat.

Darian couldn't help but wince this time. If Sarah hadn't been busy pulling at her collar again, she might have caught Ardellus's lips twitching at the corners under his mustache.

Diane sidled around the table placing the final dish in front of Sarah. She gave the young female's shoulder a squeeze. "It was so nice you could arrive in time to be a part of it." The intensity of her grasp and the tightness in her voice left Sarah certain that Diane inferred more than she'd ever say aloud.

Sure that her hair would catch fire from the heat of her cheeks, Sarah grabbed for the crystal water goblet. Just as her mouth was full of the cool liquid, Darian chuckled.

"Lamb stew. How apropos."

Water spurted clear across the table, spraying the young Regan, as Sarah choked and sputtered. Looking up and seeing the droplets running down Darian's cheeks, she flashed around the long table, napkin in hand, before Ardellus or Diane could react.

"Blessed Creator, I am so sorry." It was Darian's face she was blotting but the Regan to whom she addressed her apology.

Ardellus seemed too stunned to respond and with a quick shake of his head returned instead to his meal. Darian seized the opportunity of his father's inattention to pull Sarah's hand momentarily onto his lap, where his own napkin hid his arousal. She gasped.

"I guess you were right about the stew," he breathed in her ear before releasing her. The rest of his response was louder. "Please, I'm fine. Eat your dinner. Then perhaps I can escort you on your walk before it gets too light."

At this Ardellus's head jerked up. Sure the comment he was about to make would be addressed to her, Sarah hurried back to her seat. They hadn't spoken since she returned hours after the promised time, but she was certain she was no longer free to continue her evening strolls. Yet it was Darian to whom he spoke.

"Have you finished the copying I gave you earlier?"

Darian jabbed his spoon into his stew, more closely resembling the little boy his father addressed him as, than the fully matured male and future Regan he was. "You handed me an entire volume of the histories earlier."

Ardellus put down his utensils and waited.

Darian capitulated and looked him in the eye. "No, sir."

"And?"

Sarah averted her eyes, knowing her presence only added to his humiliation. She could hear Darian's teeth grinding before he answered.

"I'm sorry."

Ardellus nodded. "Speaking of apologies, Sarah, Darian tells me he apologized to you. Markus confirmed this, so I hope, for both their sake, it is true."

"It is," she assured him before he asked.

"And did you ever apologize to Darian like I asked you to?"

"I…" Sarah glanced at Darian, expecting him to look away, as she had. He didn't.

"She tried, but I told her she didn't have to. Feeding me was more than enough."

"And I told her she did have to. Getting your fangs does not put you in charge of the coven, Darian."

"No, but being her mate, which I'll soon enough be, puts me in charge of her." Darian turned quickly to her to explain, as if expecting her to argue or be insulted. "At least in the eyes of the law."

"I know the laws, especially those pertaining to females." She wondered if they gleaned from her tone her feelings about most of those laws.

Seeing Ardellus's eyes narrow, she suspected he, at least, did. "Then you know where the blame and the punishment falls if you choose to disobey." His eyes flitted menacingly towards his son.

"I do." She turned in her seat to address Darian.

"Don't," he implored. "I promised you last night we'd be partners, equals."

"And we are. We are equally subject to your father's rules and to the coven laws, until such time as you are in charge and those laws can be changed. So, please, let me apologize."

He seemed both stunned and amused. "Alright then. Let's hear it."

Sarah stood. "I am very sorry that your lewd behavior

the other night caused me to lose my otherwise even temper. I should not have matched your crassness with my own, but rather called out for a warrior and left it in the hands of our ancient and coveted laws. Although it would have been tragic to see your bloodline come to an end after the castration that historically has been the punishment for such unwarranted advances on a female of my standing, it would have been the proper response. So I hope you can accept my apologies." With a deep curtsy to Darian and then Ardellus, she retook her seat.

"Brilliantly put. I accept. And on behalf of my, um, bloodline," Darian's voice shook with held-back laughter as he glanced at his lap, "I thank you."

Her boldness exhausted, Sarah turned timidly to Ardellus. The Regan ran a hand through his hair before addressing her.

"That response sounds an awful lot like one your father would give to me."

"Yes, Regan, I think my father would have enjoyed that response," Sarah answered in a tone as calm as his own, "although, I imagine my mother would scold me for including the castration bit, saying it was unbecoming of a female to mention such things."

Darian's laughter was no longer silent, although the way it shook his broad frame seemed to pain him. Ardellus shot him a glare before addressing them both.

"If my striking arm weren't so tired from earlier today, I'd do more than scold the two of you."

Sarah's eyes darted to Darian's, but he didn't appear worried. He motioned for her to look back at his father whose tight, thin lips quirked into what might be considered a grin.

"As it is, I will settle for eating the rest of my dinner in silence. So I would ask that you take your walk well outside my range of hearing. You are excused, both of you."

Sarah was stunned. She offered a quick and sincere apology as well as a thank you before standing. Darian did nothing of the sort. He flashed to the door, his pain temporarily forgotten.

"Darian." Ardellus stopped him before he could escape. "Have her back in the house and yourself back in my office copying those histories well within the hour. Are we clear?"

Darian flashed him a fang-filled grin. "As a full moon, Father."

Sarah looked back one more time to see the Regan shaking his head before Darian yanked her out of the room by her wrist.

3. Special Victims Unit:
Part 2

Sarah laughed remembering it all. Cormelia and Vivian laughed along with her. Ellie on the other hand appeared as surprised as Alex felt.

"Darian hates that expression. He nearly took off Rocky's head for responding to him that way the other night."

Alex sat up from where she had settled in with her head on Vivian's tiny cool lap. "You listened to that entire story, and that's what you want to comment on?"

Ellie sneered at her. Alex ignored it and turned back to Sarah.

"First I want to know where wise-ass Sarah went. She sounds like fun." Vivian pinched her. "Right. I mean, not that you're not fun now, just…" Alex's comment hung for a moment, but Sarah remained unruffled.

"I wasn't doing it to be fun or funny. I was doing it to gain their respect. My mother, like most females of both species at the time, felt dignity was synonymous with blind obedience. My father was wise enough to see that true dignity came from being principled and strong enough to say so. Darian was easily won over to this thinking. As my story proves, he's always respected strength, in both genders. It wasn't until he'd led the coven for a few years, when he began to truly understand his father's insistence on a certain level of deference, as well."

Alex knew what Sarah was getting at. It wasn't her strong will, but her unwillingness to occasionally bend it that caused Alex trouble with the Regan. As the heat crept up her face, Sarah smiled.

"Don't feel too bad. I assure you it took me the better part of that first century to strike a balance of boldness and grace that pleased his father."

Recalling her own interactions with the stern Elder Regan, Alex's blush deepened. "You had to have had some charm over Ardellus. I nearly got my mate killed for calling his son a chauvinistic pig, something that would have been impossible had your 'Thoroughly Modern Male' actually changed coven laws regarding females. I can only imagine what he and Darian would have done had I threatened to have someone chop off his—"

When her pinching stopped working, Vivian tried gagging her instead. With a hand clamped over Alex's mouth, Vivian gave her one exasperated headshake before addressing Sarah.

"The human might take more than a century to find that balance."

"You can't balance boldness and dignity when all you have to work with is classless stupidity," Ellie mumbled.

Alex had a few classless retorts, but Vivian wisely kept her hand in place.

"Girls, please." It wasn't Sarah this time, but Cormelia who pleaded with them to stop. "This group is about helping one another, building strength together—not tearing each other to pieces. If you must be hateful, hate those who've hurt you, not others who've been hurt the same." As soft-spoken as she was, Cormelia had a way of making Alex listen. She seemed to affect the others similarly, as the atmosphere of the room returned to a more somber one.

After a moment's pause, Alex thought she heard Ellie apologize. She didn't remind her that she wasn't a vampire able to hear such a weak apology. Instead, when Vivian dropped her hand, she whispered one in return.

She then turned to Cormelia. "Do you hate them? All of them?"

Alex wondered what they knew about the ball, about the Vengatti she let go free because she couldn't bring herself to hate them simply because they were supposed to be the enemy. Would they trust her sense enough to believe they weren't all monsters? Would she be welcomed back once they knew? In that moment of questioning, she realized it would bother her if she wasn't able to return.

Cormelia's response was somewhat reassuring. "I don't hate all of them, but I can't help hating the males who were there that night. Not that hating them has helped me heal. In fact, I suspect it's kept me from a lot of good in my life." She stopped and smiled at Alex. "Like falling in love."

"I thought Markus was to blame for that. It seems too coincidental that so soon after he's out of your hair, you've found a partner and fallen for each other so quickly."

Cormelia laughed. "Well, it's true that I've known Hayden for a while, and maybe it was only a matter of time before I approached Markus about finding another feeding arrangement. But honestly, I think I needed to see him fall in love first. I needed proof that it was possible to feel so happy again."

"You also lost your lover to the Vengatti?" Alex asked, overwhelmed by the emotions she sensed from Cormelia.

The female looked back at her surprised. "No, Alex. I lost my best friend, the same night Markus lost his first love."

Alex had been told that it was Cormelia who had broken the news to Markus, but she'd always assumed the female simply had the misfortune of finding Alia's remains.

"You were there. You were attacked as well."

"Yes."

"And you survived."

"Because they let me. Because they wanted someone who could testify to Markus and to the future Regan, whom they sought revenge on, that Alia's murder was neither quick nor painless."

It took Alex a moment to remember to breathe. Waves of pain washed over her. She physically ached with what she sensed from Cormelia—and from herself. Thinking of Markus being hurt so deeply, worrying that some day it would be her fault, her life he mourned, was crushing her. When she finally spoke, her chest ached with the effort it took.

"Did you ever tell Markus what you witnessed, the details of it?"

Cormelia shook her head. "The details would have destroyed him. He would have been consumed by rage and revenge. I refused to give the Vengatti what they wanted. The truth has been the only thing I've ever refused Markus." She exchanged a quick look with Sarah who nodded, before finishing. "Darian didn't give me the choice to refuse, but he gave me his word that he'd never tell his friend the whole of it. He's the only one I ever told, the only one I will ever tell."

"So much for him being the defender of females," Ellie spat.

Alex came to the Regan's defense before anyone else had the chance.

"He didn't do it to cause Cormelia pain. He did it to cause himself pain, because he thought he deserved it, because he feels Alia's death was his fault—at least as much as any Vengatti atrocity can be someone else's fault."

Sarah and Cormelia nodded, but Alex sensed their surprise. They hadn't known Darian had shared such a personal and painful story with her. Ellie, not knowing the story, understood even less.

"He told me the night after the ball how something he had done had led the Vengatti to seek revenge on him and Markus. Actually, he was telling Ellie's brother Nathan so he'd understand that his mistake, even if justified, could have had repercussions reaching far beyond what he could have predicted." Alex paused and caught Ellie's gaze. She wanted Ellie to be clear that she knew her mistake, for which Ellie suffered, was as damaging as Nathan's. Alex had no way of knowing that the information she shared with another coven member would be used against her or against Ellie and Rocky. Then again, had she followed the safety precautions put in place to protect her from such things, she never would have met the traitor. And Ellie never would have joined the SVC. She tried once again to apologize. "I wish he had told me sooner, Ellie. I wish Nathan and I both could have learned that lesson the easy way."

"I do too." It wasn't a rebuke, but a desire too late to be fulfilled.

The five of them sat quiet for a moment. Ellie was staring into the fire. Sarah was squeezing Cormelia's hand with one hand; her other moved in small circles over her pronounced belly. Vivian was rubbing Alex's back. Alex didn't remember hunching over to fight the pain of her sense, but that was where she found herself as Vivian's contact soothed her. Alex wanted to repay their generosity, not just Vivian's, but all of theirs.

She released a soothing ripple of calm, slowly, subtly, not enough to risk rocking any of them from their pain, but enough to ease it. Vivian felt it first, since she was in physical contact with the Seer.

"You don't have to do that," Vivian said pulling back her hand.

"I want to."

"No." Cormelia had slid her hand out from Sarah's and leaned over with some urgency evident in her expression. "That's not why we asked you here, Alex."

"I know." She never would have accused these females of using her for her gift. "But I'm here. And I want to help."

"And we want your help, and we want to help you in return, but not that way." Cormelia squeezed her thigh. The gesture was meant to be comforting, but the emotions it shot into Alex only emphasized what Cormelia said next. "These feelings are too deep, too intense to manipulate permanently. Easing them temporarily would only remind us of their severity when they return. We all have other ways of regulating our emotions."

"For some of us it doesn't even involve loud, frequent sex." All eyes shot to Ellie, but when she gave

Alex a playful wink, behind which Alex sensed no hostility, Alex wagged her brows in return.

She turned to the others. "Sorry. The whole 'gifted' thing can go to my head some nights. I still struggle with the difference between my wanting to use my power on others versus when others actually want or need me to."

Vivian laughed. "Well, assuming you figure that out sometime in the next century or two, you'll still be a good hundred years ahead of our other gifted coven member."

Alex chuckled along with the others. Spinning in the love seat, she crossed her legs in front of her, facing Vivian.

"Since I already brought the Vengatti into the conversation by questioning Cormelia, I think it'd be appropriate to hear your story now. I'm dying to know how someone so smart ended up with Sage for a partner. Please tell me there was a head injury involved."

"Mine or his?" Vivian raised a thin dark brow. Her short hair and porcelain complexion along with her petite size differed as much from her partner as their personalities. There had to be some explanation for their long-lasting relationship.

"Whichever will explain for a couple centuries-long lapse of judgment on your part."

"Oh, Creator save me if we ever last that long. I've only been with Sage about a century, though I suppose that's long enough to warrant concerns for my sanity."

"But Rocky once told me Sage was around two-hundred seventy-eight. Who was his partner before you two met?"

"A question many females in the coven would love to *know* the answer to. But as he's the only Knower, I guess most of them can only hope for the best."

Vivian mocked Alex's confusion.

"I know you're not that thick, girl. He was a male who repelled females, more due to his charming personality than his marked brows. He also had an intense need for essence due to his power and the many injuries he sustained being hunted for it. Most importantly, he has a means of wiping others' memories. Put it together, and what to do you get?"

"At best, a serial fang-flipper, from the sounds of it." Ellie sounded as disgusted as Alex felt. What had come to her mind was closer to rapist, but Sage, despite his many faults, didn't fit that category. At least the Sage Alex knew now.

Alex had mixed feelings for Sage, who she both bonded and butted heads with due to the similarities of their gifts. Sarah, who too often was the referee between their 'love spats,' as she teasingly called them, knew this. She understood their teasing stemmed from a difficult but deep relationship, so when she saw Alex struggling with Vivian's words, she spoke up.

"Vivian, Ellie's right. When you explain it like that, it sounds like Sage forced females into feeding him. You, of all females, know that's not true."

"True, I fed him by choice. I didn't, however, give him permission to mess with my head afterwards. He knows I still hold a grudge about that one; my persistence is part of what he loves about me. As for being a fang-flipper, I'll forgive him that one given the circumstances."

"Fang-flipper?" It was the second time one of them used the unfamiliar term. Now that Alex wasn't worried about Sage being some perverted sexual predator, she was curious about this lesser transgression he seemed to have committed.

Ellie chimed in to explain. "The vampire equivalent of a playboy. Their motto: never drain the same vein twice."

Vivian giggled, but Sarah and Cormelia had the class to restrain themselves. Alex was unsure how to digest this. She had only recently begun feeding regularly from Markus, a necessity of her strengthening gift that had taken them all by surprise. Still, it was clear from the very first time they exchanged even a mouthful of essence how intimate an act it was. She knew plenty of girls in high school or college who thought little of a one-night stand. Honestly, if her strengthening gift hadn't kept her from the parties that usually led to such trysts, she couldn't say for sure that she never would have had one herself. But feeding was so much more. Exchanging essence was the equivalent of letting your partner taste your very soul. Sharing that like a cheap bottle of booze with anyone willing to take a swig seemed…

"Disgusting. He's a pig—or he was, at least." Alex shook her head trying to dislodge the images that accompanied this new knowledge about her mentor.

"Maybe. Maybe not." Vivian shrugged. "We all have our reasons for doing things that may or may not seem right to others."

Her gaze bore into Alex. Vivian knew. Whether Sage had told her or Sarah had, Alex didn't know, but it was clear that Vivian had learned about what Alex did at the ball. Alex probed with her sense wanting desperately to know if Vivian held it against her—the way she sensed Darian, Sage, Ellie, and even Rocky did, despite their attempts not to.

Her chest loosened when she sensed, through all the other conflicting emotions in the room, Vivian's understanding. Understanding bred from experience.

Lauren Grimley

4. Rules and Recollections:
Vivian & Sage's Story

Bristol, Massachusetts, 1902

Clutching the letter in her hand, Vivian fought hard to keep her expression neutral. The Regan had made it clear that his approval was provisionary. Any abuse of the freedom he had just granted her and her sister would lead to their immediate departure on the first ship back to Ireland. She suspected dancing across the grand lobby of the Rectinatti club, waving the separation approval, wearing her widest grin might be construed as an abuse. So she remained stoic as she waited for her sister to pull herself together. Standing before the Regan, even with Sarah, the future Regan's mate and the female coven members' advocate, had made Elana feel faint.

"Go on, if you're so impatient. I'll meet you back at the boarding house." Apparently her younger sister could see through Vivian's cool façade.

"Are you crazy? I just agreed to take full responsibility for anything we do or anything that happens to you. Do you know how many males Ardellus has beaten every year?" She thought they were alone in the long hallway leading between the Regan's office and the main foyer, but still she had whispered the words as if the walls had ears. When a response came from one of those very walls, both Elana and Vivian nearly slipped their skin.

"Far too many. It's about time a couple females kept us company."

Vivian recovered first as a strikingly tall male slid from the shadows of an alcove cut into the wood paneling. With his black pants, grey shirt, and the dark felt hat he wore low over his shaggy blond bangs, he had camouflaged himself among the shadows. It was only as he passed by one of the gas-lit sconces that the flames illuminated his face enough for her to see his dark brows marked with the two scar-like lines.

"It's rather rude to insert yourself in someone's conversation. Don't you *know* that?"

The Knower yawned dramatically, patting his hand over his mouth. "It seems you're a little *short* on originality." By this point he had reached the spot along the wall where Vivian stood by her sister's side. As he towered over her, Elana held a hand to her mouth to hide her tittering.

"At least one of you has a sense of humor." The Knower smiled at her. Elana blushed and began tugging at her curls. "Are you okay? I could walk you home if you'd like. I'm done patrols for the night."

"She's perfectly fine, thank you." Vivian glared up at him to make it absolutely clear *she* was neither intimidated nor charmed by him. The last thing she needed, less than five minutes after leaving the Regan's office, was for word to get back to him or her father that she and Elana were seen mingling with the coven's most notorious lecher.

"If you were really concerned about either of their opinions, you wouldn't have sought independence."

Vivian startled, but collected herself immediately. She averted her eyes, grabbed Elana's hand, tugging her off the bench on which she sat, and swept down the hall.

"You're right, perhaps," she called over her shoulder, "but I do care what other members of the coven think of us. And they don't think much of you and your feeding habits."

"Oh, it's my feeding habits they take issue with? And here I was thinking they were concerned I would somehow pluck their deepest, nastiest secrets from their heads if I were to accidentally brush up against them in a crowded hallway." The Knower brusquely pushed past Vivian, touching his arm to her shoulder, though there was plenty of room for him to pass.

She was about to hurl another insult at his back when Elana tugged on her arm.

"Stop."

"Please, Elana, I'm sure after a couple centuries of philandering, he's grown a thick skin."

"No, it's not..."

By the time Vivian turned to see what stopped her, Elana was half way to the granite floor. Vivian managed to flash her hand underneath her sister's head as the first of Elana's dark brown curls spilled onto the cold stone. She was lightly slapping Elana's pasty cheeks when a deep chuckle alerted her to the Knower's return.

"Looks like you'll be needing that escort home, after all. Unless, of course, *you* plan on carrying her? I'd hate to further damage her with my vile reputation."

Vivian would have liked nothing more than to deny him, but there was no way she could lug Elana home and, as it was nearing sunrise, there was no one else around to ask for help. The chances of her sister coming to and being strong or coherent enough to walk herself across the city before dawn were slim. Besides, the fact that the Knower had come back to help after she'd so strongly rebuked him was somewhat redeeming.

"Sage."

"Excuse me?"

"My name—it's Sage, unless you're fond of being referred to as female or mill girl." Without waiting for her permission, he scooped up Elana.

Vivian had been busy trying to read his intentions, once again making eye contact, completely forgetting the insight that provided him. Despite the intrusion, he had a point.

"Sorry, *Sage*. I'm Vivian, and the limp rag you're holding is my little sister, Elana."

Sage started to a side exit, avoiding the main lobby. "Little?" He tried to keep a straight face.

"Younger," Vivian corrected. "My mother contests that the Creator realized after I was born that she went too heavy on the strength and too light on the size and tried to reconcile it with her second young. I'm not sure what good long legs do, if they're constantly collapsing under you, but judging by the looks the men at the mill give her, I may be alone in that opinion."

Sage stopped by the door to allow Vivian to hold it open for him. "Human males aren't known to be the best judges of such things; they have limited senses, remember." As he passed, he kept his eyes on her. He didn't seem to be trying to hear her thoughts, but the look was still searching. She was glad when they both stepped outside onto the dark Bristol streets, glorified mud puddles after the first thaw following a snowy winter. Walking a step or two ahead of him, she began to lead him across town to the boarding house where she shared a room with Elana. With the excuse of having to focus on avoiding the deepest of the muck-filled ruts, she could avoid looking at the warrior and not be so acutely aware of his scrutinizing.

They walked in silence while they were still on the main road where a handful of others were still out despite the late hour. Elana swooned in and out of consciousness, but remained mostly unaware of her surroundings. When Vivian led Sage down a smaller side street, he broke the silence.

"So why'd you do it?"

Vivian didn't have to ask to what he was referring. She still squeezed the letter granting her and her sister's independence in her fist. It was rare for females to ask for and be granted such freedom. In the past it was a right reserved for sonless widows. But the coven was still in transition after moving to America in the middle of the last century. The Vengatti vampires had decided to emigrate from famine-stricken Ireland in search of the healthier and more plentiful food supply offered by the New World's growing population. The Rectinatti dutifully followed to thwart them as best they could. Some Rectinatti families, tired of the constant danger posed by protecting the humans, never made the move. Others had moved on to form smaller covens in other parts of the country. Still others, like Vivian's parents and grandparents, had immigrated but later decided to move back to Ireland, a few even returning to their ancestral Italy. If the newly settled coven was to continue to thrive, some allowances needed to be granted—even to females.

"We were born here. The main coven is here. We can't contribute as the Creator intended if we're dragged back across the Atlantic."

She turned in time to see Sage roll his eyes. "I was on guard outside Ardellus's office. I heard the reason you gave him. I'm asking your real reason."

"That is my real reason. There are more opportunities here—for jobs, for mates." She blushed as she gave this last reason, a reaction she didn't understand. Their kind relied on mating for survival, not just of the species, but for individual needs, as well. Yet, for some reason, thinking about those needs in the Knower's presence made her uncomfortable.

Sage shook his head. "If you wanted to mate so badly, your father could have arranged one before he left."

"I'm not sure how old you are, but arranged matings are terribly out of fashion."

"You spend too much time around the human girls you work with. What's fashionable in their world will take a good century to catch on in ours—especially in terms of female's rights."

"Fine, maybe I just don't trust my father's judgment." Vivian had stopped to glare at him.

Sage adjusted his hold of Elana.

"You think he's a coward."

Vivian was still reeling from her father's decision to return to Ireland, a land now virtually free of Vengatti. A decision he made when talk of mandatory service for males was first mentioned.

"He ran. That's what cowards do."

Sage's expression flashed with something Vivian couldn't comprehend. She stepped back instinctively.

"It depends what you're running from and what you run to." His voice was tight. She guessed the reason behind it.

"Maybe when you left whatever or whoever, you had honorable intentions. My father was just afraid, and he was willing to let the Vengatti win rather than face that fear. I'm not."

The quiet of the mid-March night was shattered with Sage's barking laughter.

"I don't find it funny."

"No, of course, you're right." Sage turned serious. "In fact, I'm sure the lead warrior will want to schedule you and lion heart, here, for training immediately. As independent females, it's only fair you serve your family's time on patrols."

Vivian's eyes widened, then she saw the twinkle in his grey-blue eyes. He was laughing again—at her.

"Laugh all you want. Not all battles are fought with blades and fangs."

"All battles with the Vengatti are, at least all of those we've ever won." Sage turned to her. His seriousness not feigned this time. "Don't let your courage or your freedom cloud your judgment. Your father's fear may or may not have breached the boundary of cowardice, but a little fear will keep you and your sister alive."

He waited for her acknowledgment, as if he had a right to demand her obedience, as if he cared enough to demand it. Could this advice come from the same male who had supposedly sucked essence from half the unmated females in Bristol? The same male who seemed to accept being shunned by the majority of the coven like a badge of honor?

His face darkened. She realized he had likely heard these comments in her head. She nodded quickly and turned into a narrow lane, a cut-off between two of the mills. They were less than half a mile from the boarding house. This awkward trip was nearly over.

"Stop."

Sage used his hip to shove her against the brick

building. She hadn't seen him do it, but he had moved Elana onto his right shoulder and had drawn a dagger with his free left hand. His eyes grew dark, the blue clouded over into ominous grey as he scoured the passage. Vivian could see him sniffing for the scent that had undoubtedly set off his reaction.

"It's old," she said, not bothering to keep her voice down. "We catch it every now and then, especially after bad weather. This is the shortest route from the main streets to the mills. Even the Vengatti don't like the snow, apparently."

He spun on her. "Are you daft, girl?"

The old Irish expression made him sound as ancient as her father. She rolled her eyes the same way she would have at him.

Sage looked as though he would have liked to hit her, had both his hands not been occupied. Vivian shrugged it off.

"We only come this way a couple times a month and always in a group."

"Of females as brave as her," Sage adjusted Elana on his shoulder, "and as big as you? That's assuring—wait, no. The word I wanted was asinine."

Vivian bristled. If he thought he could speak to her like that without an equally rude response, he was mistaken.

"Go to hell." She stood on her tiptoes to spit the words as close to his face as she could come.

Sheathing his knife, he seized her chin.

"I have personally carried the remains of female victims of the Vengatti back to their families. Nothing gets more hellish than that."

Without warning the images flashed across her mind, of a bloody snow bank, a warrior's boot kneeling next to ashes in the chilling outline of a small body, a huge hand scooping them into a dark felt hat, a mother's keening cry as she took in what remained of her child. It was the warrior's memory. Only it was in her mind.

"Stop it! Enough!" She slammed her toe into his shin. The onslaught of images stopped as abruptly as it began. "You're a bastard and a bully. No wonder no female stays with you."

His face came into focus again as she brushed away her tears. Tears she realized were caused not only by the images from his memory, but by the remembered pain— his pain. She searched his eyes for what the rest of his hardened expression hid, but he looked away.

"I may be both, but that's not why I did it, and it doesn't change the order I'm giving you: stay out of alleys like this. That clear?"

Vivian could have argued that he had no authority to give her such an order. She could have demanded an apology and threatened to report him to the lead warrior for using his gift against her in such a horrific manner.

Instead she nodded. And when he continued down the lane, left hand on the handle of his weapon, she followed in silence.

"You can't come in."

"Excuse me?" Sage had walked directly to the door of the correct boarding house. Vivian didn't ask if he had followed their scents or correctly guessed it was the one she and her sister resided in, since it was the only one owned and operated by a coven member. Either way, he was annoyed that she blocked his path.

"This is a girls-only boarding house—no men allowed."

Sage scoffed. "You're technically no longer a 'girl', and I've never been a man."

Vivian sighed and dropped her voice. "Billius can't have one set of rules for his human boarders and another for us. It would make us a little conspicuous."

"Billius begs the lead warrior for extra patrols in the area on a monthly basis. He won't have much to say about the scent of a warrior inside." Sage pushed past her and opened the door. Vivian ducked under his elbow to check the long hallway leading to their room for any other girls. Seeing it clear, she flashed down to the last door and held it open for them.

With Elana in his arms, Sage ambled down the dark corridor slower than Vivian had ever seen a human, never mind a vampire, move. He was doing it to irritate her. It worked.

When he finally walked into the small room, he wore a smug grin.

"Hers is the top bunk." She pointed to the two small beds on the left wall.

Sage lifted Elana easily onto the bed. She opened her eyes enough to mumble a thank you before drifting off again. Vivian sighed and shook her head, at which Sage chuckled.

"Rethinking that?" He motioned to the paper now in the pocket of her dress.

"No," she answered quickly. Although as his memory, now hers, flashed into her thoughts again, she couldn't repress a shudder.

"Sorry about that." Sage had been watching her, but he mumbled his apology at the floor. "When I'm pissed...I can't always control it. Or I don't always want to," he admitted with a smirk as he looked up. "I can take it back."

"No." Vivian recoiled. Seeing his jaw set, she realized this was likely the reaction half the coven had every time he entered a room. She considered what a lonely existence that would be. For the second time, she felt sympathy for him. She clarified. "It's a...useful reminder."

"Right." His tone implied he liked her compassion even less than her revulsion. He turned to glance around the room. She was sure, had he spread his arms, he could have touched the two longest walls. The space was too tiny to ever be tidy. Vivian blushed realizing everything from her undergarments to the childhood doll she still kept was out in the open for this warrior to see. He was clearly cataloging the lot, so she was surprised by his off-topic comment.

"How do you feed?"

"Pardon me?" she gasped.

He chuckled. "The females who live here. If you're not allowed male visitors, how do you *all* feed."

"Oh. Well, most of us live with a sister or close friend with whom we exchange essence. Others, I suppose, meet partners elsewhere."

He raised a brow. "You *suppose*? You told the Regan you're thirty-seven. You mean to tell me—"

"I don't mean to tell you anything, because it's none of your business." Vivian looked down and straightened her skirts to be sure she didn't inadvertently tell him through her thoughts.

"A little hypocritical from someone who's made it very clear that she's kept tabs on my feeding habits, don't you think?"

"The fact that the whole coven seems to know your poor feeding habits is not my fault."

"No, clearly it's mine. I guess I need to stop making public announcements at the club," he sneered. His face held the same expression it had when he had agreed to her insults of bully and bastard. It hinted at something, something softer than the hard shell he exuded. She'd never been particularly curious, but his was a mystery she wanted to solve. Unlike him, though, she had no means of reading further into it. It was her frustration over this that left her mocking him.

"Do you expect me to feed you now? In exchange for your help? Is that why you're sticking around?"

He didn't find her funny. His fists clenched by his side.

"Thank you for confirming that you're as arrogant and small-minded as the rest of them. You almost had me thinking otherwise."

His words stung. His opinion ought not to have mattered, but it did. He was nearly out the door before she caught her breath enough to respond, anger trumping hurt.

"I didn't realize you were so picky."

Her back slammed against the far wall. Sage had torn across the room and had her pinned. His massive body pressed against her slight frame. She could feel his fangs brush against her neck.

"I didn't realize you were so eager."

"You're hurting me."

"Some females like it rough, but you wouldn't know, I *suppose*."

She responded with a knee aimed at his groin. He shifted as soon as the thought crossed her mind and well before she made contact.

"That's not fair!" She twisted to break free. "And without my permission, it's also illegal."

Sage scoffed. He dropped her hands from where he had them pinned.

"I've got my fangs practically in your artery, and

you're protesting the legality and *fairness* of my reading your thoughts? That's a new one. And I assure you, there's nothing fair about my so-called gift."

"I know. You get to know everything about us, and we get to know nothing about you. And people hate you, or more accurately, fear you because of it. But did you ever consider that you're partly to blame for that? You hide behind those lines." She pointed to his brows. "You get pissed when someone feels sympathy for you and bitter when they don't. You can't have it both ways. That's not fair, not to someone who's trying to know the real you, and not to yourself."

A grin played on his lips as he continued to listen to her thoughts. She had done it again. She averted her eyes, breaking the contact. Too late.

"If you're done," she said glaring up at him, "you can show yourself out."

"You were serious about feeding me. Or at least seriously considering it. You're crazier than I am, you know that?"

"Ugh." Her tiny fists balled at her sides. She had just explained how she didn't *know* anything about him, yet every time she turned around, he'd plucked something else from her head. She wanted to punch him, to scratch at his face, to throw him on the bed and suck an ounce of essence, of knowledge, from his veins. Blood pooled suddenly under the surface of her skin. She glanced up to see if he had somehow heard that thought too, despite the absence of eye contact or physical touch. She released her held breath when she saw he hadn't.

He was shrugging, apparently unwilling to apologize twice in one evening.

"I usually have better control." He chuckled. "No, actually, I don't. But normally I don't need it. Few coven members look me in the eye the way you do, even those who know me and trust me." His voice had softened at this last statement. He wasn't mocking her again. He'd meant it, appreciated it, even.

"Would I do it less or more if I knew you?" Vivian blurted aloud the question she was really asking herself.

His smile was warm and genuine. "I guess we'll never know." He gave her a slight bow, tipped his hat, and headed back for the door.

Spring washed right into summer that year. The constant rain, which followed a snowy winter, had washed out half the roads in Bristol. By mid-July Vivian had given up hope of ever being completely dry or mud free. Elena had passed off her sister's sour mood to her dislike of being dirty and her abhorrence of the never-ending laundry.

"For Creator's sake, I'll wash your stockings tonight," she cried over the rain one evening. Vivian had stopped at the entrance to their usual shortcut on the way home from visiting a widowed aunt who lived on the other side of the city. Elena had thought her reluctance to enter was due to the deep puddles that riddled the alleyway.

Vivian had told her sister about the memory the Knower had planted in her mind, but hearing it was different than seeing the images. She saw the blood stained snow bank every time she walked past one of Bristol's darker cut-throughs.

"Bastard," she mumbled into the driving rain. What right did he have to tell her what to do? Something tugged at the corners of her memory. *My life, my rules.* That wasn't exactly right, though the sentiment was the same.

"C'mon, let's go." She grabbed her soaked skirt with

one hand and Elana's slippery forearm with her other. They flashed down the alley and continued at full speed until they stood at the door to the boarding house. Between the rain and the dark, no human could possibly have noticed them, and it felt good not to act human for a change. Breathless and laughing, they threw open the door. Elana ducked inside and Vivian made to follow when movement in her peripheral vision froze her.

A shock of blond hair on a shaking head at the corner they'd just burst out of?

She had wiped the water from her eyes and he was gone. Never there to begin with, more likely.

This time, though, she was certain she was seeing him through the grimy rain-spotted panes of the mill windows. He was walking on the dark street below, with a smaller, slighter male by his side, another warrior perhaps. When he turned around looking in her direction, the crate she'd been holding crashed to the floor. Dozens of spent wooden spindles cascaded across the dusty boards. All of the nearby girls not working a loom rushed to her rescue, sweeping them back in the box. The mess was cleaned up nearly as quickly as it was created, but not quick enough to escape the notice of the night foreman.

"If you're too delicate to do the work, there are a dozen other girls who can."

Henry Wainslow was the son of the mill manager. His weak jaw and soft torso didn't make him intimidating in stature, yet with his position of authority and nasty disposition he managed to bring one of the girls to tears nearly every night. If he thought standing over Vivian, one of the few workers he could tower over, would elicit the same response, he was sorely mistaken.

"Can those dozen other girls carry their own

weight—literally?" Vivian stacked the refilled crate on not one other, as the men sometimes did, but on two other full boxes. The stack was nearly as tall as her five-foot frame, yet she lifted it with ease. She started to the back wall where the spindles were stacked to be collected by the boys and brought back to the spinning room. She ought to have left it at that, but her temper got the better of her. The comment slipped out as she passed him.

"Can you for that matter?"

There were a few gasps from the other girls. Some of the females from the coven glared at her reproachfully as she walked by publicly displaying the strength they were sworn to hide. As if being fired and blacklisted weren't enough, Vivian now imagined the Regan's reaction when word got back to him.

When she returned to her loom, though, Henry was gone. All the other workers, save Elana, whose panic was evident, had returned to their tasks.

"It's okay," she whispered across the din, knowing her sister could still hear. "He can't hurt us, not really." She flashed her fangs and winked. Elana returned a watery smile.

At the changing of shifts, Henry reappeared, as he always did. Vivian's apprehension grew as she saw him conversing in angry whispers with his father. Over the noise of the machines, even her enhanced hearing wasn't enough to decipher their words, but Henry's smirk as they concluded didn't bode well.

As the nighttime crew of workers traded off responsibilities with the larger daytime crew and headed for the exits, William Wainslow, the mill manager and Henry's father, put up a hand to stop them.

"Two of our daytime shift won't be in. We'll need at least one of you to stay and work their looms."

It was against labor laws to keep workers longer than their already grueling twelve-hour shift. Everyone in the room knew it. But with two of Bristol's mills already having closed up and gone south, and another rumored to be next, no one lucky enough to be employed was foolish enough to mention this to the boss.

Vivian felt her coworkers' eyes landing on her in rapid succession. It would have been wise for her to make amends to Henry by volunteering. It would have been right for her, as one of the younger vampires, to step in for the others, many of whom were nearing the age that a daytime shift in the windowed room would be painful, if not dangerous. Yet when she saw Elana standing next to her, her quivering knees obvious beneath her skirt, Vivian remained silent.

As she suspected, it was a vain gesture. Henry had intended all along for her to stay.

"The little one, Vivian, she'll stay. As she so aptly proved earlier, she can easily do the job of two workers."

Vivian nodded, for once keeping her comments to herself.

"I'll be back at closing to lock up for the weekend, Father." Henry stole one last look at Vivian before leaving in a swirl of lint kicked up from the floor. The smile he wore turned Vivian's stomach and left her fangs aching from the strain of keeping them retracted.

"Rachel," she spoke to the oldest and huskiest of the Rectinatti females, "will you see Elana home safely?"

The older female clucked her tongue at Vivian but wrapped a thick arm around Elana's waist as she led her to the door.

By the end of the second shift Vivian was dead on her feet. Leaning on the broom handle, she couldn't imagine any human worker making it through the day. Perhaps, though, some of her exhaustion was from a lack of essence. It wasn't that Elana didn't provide her with enough, as the younger female had begun to worry. It was more that it no longer seemed to satisfy her. Vivian was certain it was her own fault. It started the night after they'd been granted their independence. She thought the added responsibility for her sister, who Vivian knew secretly pined for their parents, was keeping her from drawing essence from Elana the way she had in the past. It was the only reason that made sense.

"All right, you lot, clear out. We're locking up." William stood by the door, keys in hand.

Vivian dumped the dustpan full of scraps of thread and balls of lint into the barrel along the wall and started for the exit. She averted her eyes as she passed the manager. A rough hand clamped her arm.

"You can't leave that barrel full over the weekend. Take it out back and empty it. Henry'll wait for you before he locks up."

Vivian glared up at the heavy-set human with the same weak jaw and small twitchy eyes as his son. She had all she could do to maintain a semblance of composure.

This was their plan all along, to keep her here, not just to work an unpaid shift, but also to provide Henry an opportunity to batter or abuse her without the possible interference of another worker. Thinking back to those girls who trembled in his presence, or the ones who left after a shift and never returned, she knew he had done it to other girls in the past. It was too well calculated to be his first time. The extra hour it had taken to clean up and shut down the machines for the weekend meant the sun had set. The alley leading to the back of the mill, where the trash was dumped to be burned and swept into the river, would be completely dark. Swelled with the recent rain, the rushing waters that powered the mills and ran behind the building would drown out the noise of her protests.

Or in this case, Henry's.

"Of course, sir. Have a nice weekend," she managed. "Perhaps I'll see you Monday." Or perhaps he'd stay home attending to his son's injuries, while she headed to the coven's club to inquire about other jobs available to females, so that she'd never have to see his sleazy face again.

William watched her warily as she carried the barrel by him with one hand, portraying no signs of the fear he likely expected. Vivian couldn't help but smile at him. She hoped having to explain away the deep bruise in the shape of her tiny hand to the police officers who would later discover the whimpering Henry, would be humiliating enough to keep William from ever partaking in his son's schemes again.

The rain had let up temporarily, leaving the mill yard quiet except for the sound of the river beyond the banks. She didn't try to be stealthy as she rounded the darkened corner carrying the barrel. She wanted Henry to know she was coming, wanted him to think he had the upper hand.

One step into the open space at the back of the mill, the barrel clattered to the slick cobblestones. Even in the thick early evening air she caught the scent. It was fresh, or it would have washed away in the day's earlier downpours. Henry had company.

"Disappointing, Henry. I ask for a meal, and you bring me an hors d'oeuvre."

Vivian didn't wait to get a closer look at the Vengatti male who spoke. She flashed back the way she came, hoping to make it to the main road before either of them realized what she was. Twenty yards from the mouth of the mill's drive she hit a patch of mud. Moving at full speed it turned into a slick beneath her tiny feet. She lost her footing, crashing onto the wet pavers, splitting her chin as it hit the ground.

She was scrambling to her feet when a heavy boot slammed onto her arm, snapping the bone like a dry twig. Vivian shrieked in agony until she was yanked to her feet, a hand clamped over her mouth. When her screams subsided, another sound echoed through the alley.

He was laughing.

"My apologies, Henry," he said as the human caught up to where the two vampires stood. "Half a Rectinatti female, a feisty one at that, will more than suffice. You won't even have a body to dispose of when I'm done. I suppose that will deprive you of your usual…entertainment, but there's always next time."

"She's…like you?" Henry couldn't bring himself to name the creature he obviously partnered with in this sick plan.

Vivian was still struggling to free herself, kicking and thrashing. Her fangs sprang and she bit through the palm of the Vengatti. He jerked his hand back.

"I'm nothing like this son of a bitch!" Vivian stomped her heal into his foot, hoping he'd loosen his grip allowing her to wriggle free.

Instead he yanked her closer and tore into the flesh on her neck. Her fighting became frantic; she was scratching, tearing, biting, at every inch of his exposed flesh. Anything to keep him from stealing her essence, her very spirit. To keep from being drained and killed. Or worse, left alive but empty, without enough essence to recover her sense of self. Each move only added to her agony as his fangs dug a deeper, wider gash in her tender throat. When she started to lose consciousness, it was almost a blessing.

Then with a snarl, he dropped her. Vivian's eyes tried to focus on the spot the Vengatti's had snapped to. She caught a glimpse of the small male she had seen with the Rectinatti Knower the previous night, a second knife leaving his hand. Then something crashed into her, sweeping her from her knees, carrying her back a dozen yards to the corner of the building. She was set on her feet and released as soon as she had steadied herself.

"Follow the human. Go around the building, then straight home. Don't wait for him—or us. Just go. We'll send Abram to the boarding house later to treat you."

The Knower spoke rapidly, while pushing her away from the two fighting vampires who blocked the shortest path to the main road. She watched, rooted to the muddy ground as the smaller warrior barely dodged blow after blow.

"He needs help." Vivian staggered forward a step.

"Not yours. Do as I say." He grabbed her uninjured arm and spun her around. "Go. Now!"

You don't know what's good for me.

She was looking in his eyes as the echo of her own voice bubbled up from somewhere deep below the surface of her thoughts. His eyes widened, and he went rigid. She didn't understand his expression.

"Sage!" The plea from the smaller warrior shook them both. Seeing his partner, blood dripping from a gash on one shoulder, spurred the Knower back into action. He flashed across the alley, knife in hand, not even bothering to look back as he ordered her one last time.

"Run, Vivian!"

'Cowards run.' 'It depends what they're running from and what they're running to.'

'Follow the human.' Henry. He must have fled when the

Rectinatti warriors arrived. Vivian careened around the corner and crashed into him. He had been crouching in the shadows watching the violence unfold. She grabbed him with her one good hand and threw him to the ground. He started to scuttle away through the mud. She stomped on his ankle, cracking his brittle human bones as easily as the immense Vengatti had broken her arm.

"Please!" he cried out. "Don't!"

"How many girls have begged the same of you or that monster you lure them to?" Vivian demanded, drawing strength from her rage.

"I won't tell the others what you are. And I'll stop, I swear—"

"How many?" She kneeled on his chest, so her fangs were clear even through the torrents of rain that had resumed sometime during the attack.

"A c-couple," he stammered.

Vivian tore at his fleshy cheek with one fang. The blood from the gash mixed with the water dripping onto him from her black locks, sending a current of red running down his pasty face.

"How many?"

"Fix. S-six," he amended as she growled again. "You would have been six."

"Why?"

Henry only shook his head. Even through the rain she could smell his fear and his tears. The display of weakness from the man who found so much joy in others' distress disgusted her, but not nearly as much as the rest of what she knew to be true, what she insisted he admit to. She tightened her grip on his neck.

"It…excites me, to watch them die."

"And after?"

Henry's terror rendered him speechless. She slashed

at his other cheek.

"What do you do to their bodies?" Vivian's voice wasn't her own. It was raw, wild, lacking all humanity. Her grasp was too tight for Henry's voice to carry, but she heard the choked confession of his foulest acts right before her thumb crushed his windpipe.

'You would have been six.'

"No. Let's go the way I sent her...just in case." His voice had an edge—the same edge she remembered from the warning he had given her about the alleys. Not anger, but...

"What the hell are you still doing here?"

Maybe anger.

He towered over where she still sat on the sodden ground on the edge of the river's bank. It was as far as she'd managed to stagger before dropping to her knees and retching.

"Sage." His partner stood twenty feet away pointing to the remains of Henry's tattered body. The human's throat had been crushed and his face bitten and bloodied beyond recognition. The warrior already had his hand on another knife, or maybe it was the same one he had thrown at the Vengatti. They wouldn't have come searching for her before killing him.

"I can't catch a scent with all this rain. Find out if she saw the second one and where he went." He nodded towards Vivian.

When the Knower knelt down and grasped her chin, she realized why the warrior hadn't addressed her. She was shaking so hard it took two hands to keep her still. The smaller warrior must have known it would be easier to pluck whatever information was needed from her head than to try to question her.

"I told you not to wait for him," Sage growled trying to force her to look at him, making his gift easier to work. "You could have been killed too."

"He's a human." As the words tumbled out, Vivian realized the gravity of what she had done.

"Not by him, by the other Vengatti who—"

For a second time that night her thoughts stopped him cold. He didn't pull away this time. Vivian didn't fight it. She knew what she had done. She knew the repercussions of her actions could be severe. But as the Knower retraced her memory of Henry's confession, she knew she'd do it again.

"Did she see?" The other warrior was peering through the dark yard impatiently.

"No." Sage stood up. He looked once between the corpse, sitting in a pool of bloodstained mud, and Vivian, whose face and hands had mostly been washed clean by the rain. "But she thought she heard him heading back to the main road. He's likely long gone. Check that it's clear. I'll stay with her."

The smaller warrior nodded and disappeared around the far corner of the building.

Vivian looked to Sage for an explanation, but he headed back to the body. When he began carrying it towards her, she panicked, scrambling to her unsteady feet. She collapsed almost immediately.

"Easy. I'm just sending the sick bastard to his final resting place." With that he hurled the body over the shrubs lining the river. The splash sounded distant in the stormy night air.

He flashed back to where she fell. "You need to feed." Despite the conviction of his statement, his brows furrowed like he was unsure of how to proceed.

"Please." The mere mention of essence left her

aching for it. Her desire derived from her injuries, her blood loss, her exhaustion—and him. Suddenly the reason behind her disheveled state over the course of the last four months was clear. It made no sense. In the one hour they'd spent together, he'd questioned her judgment, scared her, taunted her, and nearly assaulted her. Their one conversation was more of an argument. And he had walked out the minute it threatened to become something more. Yet she yearned for him now, like her body knew something her mind didn't.

"I'm sorry."

She thought he was denying her. She was startled when he came behind her to cradle her in one arm, bringing his other wrist to her mouth. He seemed to hear the internal struggle between her desire for blood and her fear of losing control the minute her fangs came out. Her mouth still tasted of Henry's flesh. Sage snapped his own fangs and pierced the skin on his wrist, quickly bringing it to her lips.

She fed deeply, frantically, at first, with no recognition of the taste or strength of the essence she took from him. With her body's initial need satiated, she began to drink more slowly, savoring the sweetness of a male's more completing essence. No, of Sage's more completing essence. It was wonderful, pure, and…familiar.

Images flooded her memory, glimpses at first. Then the words began to come and the pieces fell together until they were complete, right up until the final words he had spoken before he made them all disappear.

◦≪═╤═≫◦

"I guess we'll never know."

"Wait." She had flashed to his side as he started to leave the room that night he had first walked them home. She wanted a more satisfying response. She wanted to know—to know whether she could trust him, to know why she already seemed to trust him, to know why not knowing was driving her insane.

He didn't seem to hear these other questions in her thoughts. He was too entranced by her hand on his arm. He looked at it as if such a simple gesture was alien to him. It made her sad and angry. It also made her confident she meant what came out of her mouth next.

"You should stay. It's almost sunrise."

He shrugged. "I'll find a dark spot to sleep."

"Not one as close and safe as here."

Sage looked down at her with that unreadable expression again. She didn't bother to look aside. Her racing heart gave it all away.

"To be clear, what are you offering?"

"Something I doubt you're used to or comfortable with: a fair exchange."

He shut the door with one hand and yanked her against him with the other.

"For someone so tiny, you're awfully mouthy, you know that?"

"What are you going to do about it?" Vivian asked with one part trepidation, one part unbridled anticipation.

His face grew serious. "Only as much as you want me to."

Her voice gone, she nodded. When he still seemed unsure, she tugged him back towards the bed. What little the gesture didn't say, her thoughts, as she held his hands in hers, did. She wanted to know him, but she also just wanted him—and not only his essence.

He glanced up at the top bunk where Elana had slept peacefully through their earlier argument. He tugged her blanket over her head, just in case, then turned to Vivian with a grin that gave her goose bumps from her scalp to her toes.

"You asked for it."

He had her dress off in the space between two of her rapid heartbeats. Instead of throwing her onto the bed, as she had expected, he pushed her over onto the small desk by the door. One hand between her shoulder blades held her down firmly; her small breasts pressed into the cool wooden surface. His other hand pulled her hips back as he slid inside her. She gasped.

"Silence," he commanded with a slap that left her bottom stinging.

She started to giggle until he pounded into her with a punishing thrust of his hips. She cried out. He leaned over her squeezing both her sensitive nipples tightly between his thumb and forefinger until she couldn't help but suck in a sharp noisy breath.

"You're not a very quick learner, are you?" he whispered. "Now, hush." He silenced her with a nip on the back of her neck, which he healed by gently tickling his tongue over the teeth marks. It was torturous not to react. The bastard knew what he was doing.

His hands moved expertly over her breasts, down her back, around the front of her thighs, yet he never missed a beat as he slowly increased his rocking, moving them both towards a climax. He pulled back only when she started to moan.

"Uh-uh," he teased. She reached back to claw at him, but he grabbed her hands entwining his fingers with hers. Knowing he'd deny her until she obeyed, she bit her lip and gripped the desk crushing their hands together to keep silent. His ulterior motive became evident when she realized repressing that one reaction intensified her body's other responses. As her insides shattered, what escaped her lips was a fierce growl. Sage tugged her back by her chin-length hair allowing him to penetrate even deeper as he finally came inside her. Her legs went limp beneath her, but his body, resting on hers, kept her from collapsing.

When they both began to catch their breath, she felt his wrist press against her lips.

"Go on. It's why you really wanted me to stay, isn't it?"

"Well, half an hour ago I would have answered yes to that question, but now…"

Sage released a barking laugh, breaking his own rule. He stood up, gave her another rough slap on the rear end, and pulled her onto his lap in the wooden desk chair, before she could even protest.

"That actually hurts, you—" His wrist was on her lips again. She pushed it away and without a second's hesitation bit into his neck, sucking fervently from the vein. His essence was sweet, as pure as she expected. This was what the hard expression hid. Part of it, at least.

She took her time, making a meal of him, as their heartbeats slowed. Their sweat had nearly dried on their pale naked skin by the time she closed the puncture marks. When Sage tried to bring her wrist up to his mouth, she slapped him and shook her finger in his face.

"Oh, no you don't. My turn, my rules."

"Your turn? You've never even—"

She was holding his face in her hands, willing him to hear her thoughts, her memories, at least parts of them.

"You little tramp!" But his laughing tempered his shocked expression.

"Three partners in the seventeen years since my maturity hardly makes me a tramp." Actually, she knew plenty of coven members who'd dispute that, so she qualified her remark. "In comparison to you, anyway.

You don't think a virgin would let you take her that way on her first time?"

"I've been told that I can be exceptionally charming when I want to be," Sage replied.

"Huh, I would have thought your mind-reading would have saved you from such delusions."

"Delusions?" He jerked a marked brow.

"Maybe. Let's confirm."

Vivian was on her feet. She pulled on both his hands, leading him back to the bed. When the backs of her legs hit the frame, she pushed him onto his knees. Sitting naked before him with her thighs spread, she pointed to her femoral artery, which she knew he could hear pulsing below the surface of her skin.

"One of us has a reputation to keep up—as false as it may be." She was the one wearing the wicked grin this time.

Something flashed in Sage's eyes. He shook it off and reached for her cheeks with both hands.

She slapped him again. "No touching. Not with your hands."

He met her eyes with one dark marked brow raised.

"You don't need your gift to clarify that instruction...do you?"

As it turned out, he didn't. His tongue obeyed divinely. His fangs, however, had a mind of their own.

"Hey!" Vivian was shaken from her bliss when they pierced her neck. She pulled at his hair until he was forced to retract his fangs or rip the flesh from her throat. "I told you—"

"Does your sister feed from here?" His hand squeezed her inner thighs, one long finger trailing up her skin.

Vivian answered in a voice much too breathy and

bothered for her liking. "No, but she'll know she didn't feed from me recently."

Sage shook his head with apparent impatience. "She'll *know* whatever I want her to know."

"You're downright dangerous with that," Vivian told him, unsure how serious she ought to be.

"More than you'll ever know."

She ought to have asked about his tone of voice, about the puzzling expression that had once again appeared, but he had resumed feeding from her, caressing her, breaking all of her rules so wonderfully, she soon forgot she created them.

She awoke in the early evening when the chilled spring air sent shivers over her bare skin. Before her eyes could focus, she heard her sister's soft sleepy voice, and that of another—a male. Sage had stayed until sunset. Somehow that both surprised and thrilled her.

"You seem better now that you've had a little of your sister's essence."

"Mmm, yes, she's good to me. Lately I fear she gives more than she takes, though. I'm not sure it's ever enough."

"That explains a lot." Sage rubbed his neck.

Vivian reached across the bed and pinched his thigh as her sister asked, "What?"

"Nothing, Elana, go back to sleep." When he ducked his head under the upper bunk he grimaced. "That actually hurts, you know," he whispered, mimicking her complaint of the previous night, as he rubbed his thigh.

"I intended it to," she said with a smile he didn't return.

He had turned his back to her. He sat on the edge of the bed and tugged on his boots in a silence that said plenty.

"You're leaving."

"Yes."

She reached out and touched his arm, silently asking him what she couldn't voice. *For good?*

He seemed surprised at first that she had purposely communicated with him that way. Vivian couldn't tell whether it pleased or bothered him. When he shook it off, he put his hand over hers and turned back to look down at her with that same mysterious expression.

"For yours."

"You don't know what's good for me."

"Don't I?" he asked sardonically.

"No, not that." She ripped the sheet out from under him and clutched it to her chest. "You don't know everything, especially not what's good for *me*. Hell, I'm not even convinced you know what's good for yourself."

"Don't curse. It makes you sound cheap."

"Like all the other females you've slept with?" She was sitting up so she could glare at him, but he was back to lacing his boots.

"Exactly. But you're not like all the others." He finally faced her with an expression as angry as hers, as if everything were somehow her fault.

"No, I'm not. I'm willing to look you in the eye. I actually want to know what's behind that look you have every time you get too close to feeling something. Doesn't that count for anything?"

"Yes, not that it does either one of us any good. But I'll tell you since you want to *know* so badly. Regret. Sympathy. Sometimes even concern. That's what's behind the look."

"Just concern, not the beginnings of something else, something stronger?"

Sage laughed, but it rang hollow. "I guess we'll never

know."

"You're going to try to leave me with that again?"

"Not again." He reached forward and took her chin in his hands before she had any inkling what he was doing. "That's how I left, the first time. You were annoyed, but forgot about it when you heard Elana wake. She was weak from the fainting spells, so you fed her, just a little. She'll likely need more later tonight. But it's Sunday, so go back to sleep. Let her rest. You can celebrate your independence and curse the bloody Knower who filled your head with scary warnings of dark alleys when you wake."

When her eyes had glassed over, he dropped his hand and slipped as silently from the room as he had from her memory.

"How dare you?" Vivian pushed herself from Sage's arms and slapped him with every bit of her returning strength.

"I said I was—" He stopped when his partner reappeared by their side, fuming.

"What's going on? Did he hurt you?"

Sage seemed equally furious at his partner's accusation. "I wouldn't hurt her. Not intentionally," he added watching the tears mixed with rain dripping from her face. "I fed her, after she asked me to."

"Then why did she strike you?"

"It's none of your business, Markus."

The smaller warrior narrowed his eyes. "You're right. It's an issue for the lead warrior, not me. Be sure to include your explanation in the report you give to my father. In the meantime, I'll take her to Abram's clinic. Bring her sister to see her after you clean up the body." Markus looked back at where the corpse had been. He spun on Sage.

"Later," was the Knower's quick and forceful reply to whatever question he had heard in Markus's mind.

Vivian's knees began to quiver again. The adrenaline that had accompanied feeding and its aftermath was draining from her body like the trails of muddy water that flowed from her skirt. Sage caught her as she began to sway and scooped her easily into his arms.

"I guess I'll bring her to Abram's. You can get her sister, Elana, from Bilius's boarding house. Have her pack their things—all of them."

Markus eyed him suspiciously. Vivian was sure he was mentally relaying some message or threat, but finally he nodded in agreement and flashed back in the direction of the original attack.

Drowsy from whatever drugs Abram, the coven's physician, had given her, Vivian struggled to open her eyes. When her vision cleared and the sterile white room came into focus, she was startled by the presence of others—two others.

Elana was curled up beside her in the bed. Vivian could tell from her pasty white cheeks that her sister had not handled the news of Vivian's attack and the sight of her injuries well. She wondered sadly if this was the final blow that would send Elana scampering back to her parents and the safety of Ireland.

"She fainted, twice. When she opened the door and saw Markus, bleeding and muddy, and again when she awoke and saw your injuries. Abram's son Christo gave her nearly as strong a dose of sedatives as he gave you."

Vivian turned towards the sound of his voice, sending a searing pain through her neck, where her wound, though already healing, was still raw. Sage leaned against the wall across from her bed like a sentinel, though clearly there was no threat now that she was in the home of a prestigious coven member.

"I sent the usual guard home for the day. I figured you might have...questions."

"How are you doing that? I wasn't touching you or even looking directly at you."

Sage smirked, "I would have figured after last night, you'd be able to answer that one without my help."

"I have your essence in me." Vivian didn't understand exactly how a Knower's gift worked, but it made sense that the connection of having his own blood in her would be the same as physical touch or eye contact.

"Stronger, actually."

"So strong it restores any shared memories." She doubted he needed a connection to hear the anger in her voice.

"I rarely apologize and never twice for the same infraction. If you were smart enough to realize the trouble I was trying to save you from, you'd thank me. Then again, if you were smart, you wouldn't have fallen for me to begin with."

It was good her broken right arm had been splintered or she might have launched herself out of bed and pummeled him with both her fists. That might have covered for the fact she hadn't denied his claim. Despite everything, she knew he was right. It explained so much. Her mood for the last few months. Her inability to derive enough essence from Elana. And her rage.

"I don't think my intelligence is the problem. The issue seems to be one of strength. You've underestimated mine, if you think I'd care what the coven thinks of me being your partner. And I clearly overestimated yours. I told you the night we met that I believe running from one's problems is a form of cowardice, but you convinced me then that that wasn't always the case. Well, I'm sorry, *warrior*, but using your gift so you can run away without a trace is as cowardly as it comes."

Having exhausted her herself with her tirade, Vivian collapsed back onto the pillow and closed her eyes to catch her breath. The last glimpse she caught of Sage, his lips were pressed together in a tight white line to hide the fury evident by his elongated fangs. It was satisfying to see she'd gotten under his skin as deeply as he'd burrowed under hers. Focused on her own uneven breath, she almost didn't hear the last words he whispered.

"With the others, maybe. With you, it takes a hell of a lot more strength to walk away."

When her eyes popped open, he was gone. But not far enough. Injuries be damned, she flashed down the hall, stopping inches in front of him. She swayed but managed to steady herself.

"Maybe I didn't make myself clear, or maybe you managed to erase that part of your own memory." She reached up and grabbed *his* chin this time. "You don't get to make those decisions on my behalf. I fed from you twice now, because *I* wanted to. If I want you to leave me 'for my own good,' I'll let you know—and you'll leave, so you better hope it's not the middle of the afternoon, as it is right now."

Sage stared down at her in...disbelief? Anger? He didn't speak. He didn't move. As the seconds ticked, Vivian began to lose confidence. What if he denied her? What if he wasn't as strong as she thought he was, strong enough to believe her, strong enough to stay?

He started to laugh. "Compared to you, I'm a weak human. If I were a child-sized female in my first half-century of life, I don't think I'd be threatening one of the largest warriors in the coven—especially not if he was privy to all my indiscretions." Sage raised a brow. She should have realized from the salacious smile he wore that he was referring to her bedroom behaviors, but all she could think about was what she had done the night before.

"Is that brave or foolish?" She wondered what he'd tell Markus, the son of the lead warrior, when 'later' finally came.

"I told him the truth, because I knew he'd understand and keep it quiet. Humans like Henry Wainslow aren't the kind we're sworn to protect. Although he wished you'd have come to us earlier for help, even if you didn't know the Vengatti were involved, Markus thought facing Henry initially showed a great deal of courage. What happened after…well, he knows you had just been fed from."

"And you? What do you think?"

Sage had seen her memory and heard her thoughts. He knew lack of essence had nothing to do with what she'd done to Henry.

"I think you were quicker and kinder than I would have been." Sage ground his teeth. "I also think, no, I know that if you ever do anything that stupid from here on out, you'll wish to the Creator that you had better taste in partners."

Vivian grinned. This was clearly the closest he'd come to admitting that he had been foolish enough to fall for her, too.

"Really? And what are you going to do about it?" She began backing up when his grin returned and twisted into a devious grimace.

"I thought your memory was restored, but maybe you need a stronger reminder." He grabbed the front of her gown and spun her around, slapping her rear as hard as he had that first night.

"I thought I told you that hurts."

"You also told me you love it," he whispered into her ear as he held her close to him, careful not to jostle her arm.

"I said no such thing!" she protested, swatting back at him with her good hand.

"Who claimed you 'said' it?" Sage swept her off her feet and started back to the hospital bed wearing the widest of smiles.

"I'm going to regret this, aren't I?" She couldn't help but pout.

"Every night until you smarten up and give me the boot."

"Fine. So long as you're aware that I plan to make this partnership equally painful for you."

He placed her softly back onto the side of the mattress not occupied by her sleeping sister. When he stood erect his fangs were out. He pushed one of them slowly, deliberately into his bottom lip until it bled. Then he licked the flesh clean with a single flick of his venom soaked tongue, before he answered.

"Promise?"

Lauren Grimley

5. Special Victims Unit:
Part 3

"I owe you an apology, Alex. Following that story, I'm very glad it's you and Markus, not Sage and Vivian, in the bedroom next to mine."

After Ellie's earlier implication that Alex was self-centered, she was tempted to point out that it was Ellie who had brought the conversation back to her and Rocky after both Sarah and Vivian's tales. Recalling Sarah's request that Alex be more understanding of Ellie, however, she kept quiet. There was a reason Ellie was hyper-focused on her relationship with Rocky. It was the easiest, happiest part of her life right now, the one topic she could talk about without resurfacing her pain or fear. Alex wondered if maybe Ellie would tell them the parts of that story Rocky never had. But that would have to wait.

Vivian's story, even more than Sarah's, seemed far from complete. Alex had a hundred questions, but one in particular ate at her.

"What about Henry's father, William Wainslow? The bastard helped. Did you go back for him?"

Vivian flashed her an understanding smile and patted her knee, while Sarah shook her head.

"What?" she challenged the Regan's mate, perhaps unwisely.

"You sound a little too much like a warrior some days," Sarah answered matter-of-factly. "And that's not a compliment," she added when Alex squared her shoulders and started to grin.

She shrugged and turned to Vivian, hoping for a more satisfying response.

"I was full of rage that night, but I'm not a warrior, Alex. I wanted nothing to do with going back there. Sage, though, thought along the same lines as you. Luckily Markus forbade him to do anything that would have gotten us both in hot water."

Alex's eyes narrowed. Hundred-year time gap aside, her mate was going to hear about this one.

"It's okay. Your mate has other, sometimes more painful, and often more effective, means of getting others to do what he wants. He paid a visit to the elder Wainslow. He made it clear what he was and that he'd be watching William to assure no other girl from his mill ever came to harm again. He apparently made enough unannounced appearances—popping up all over Bristol—to terrify the man into an early retirement. The mill closed less than two years later, and William rarely left his Bay Side home in the decade before he died, quite young, of heart failure."

Alex nodded. "Good. And Markus kept his word, so Ardellus never found out?"

"Markus always keeps his word and is quite good at keeping his mouth shut, too, which I'm very grateful for considering what he and Cormelia have overheard in the last century."

"She's referring as much to their fights as to their other...interactions," Cormelia teased.

Alex wanted to ask about that, too, not to be nosy, but because Vivian and Sage's relationship had many of the same hurdles that her and Markus's did, one of which worried her even after their mating.

"Most of your fights...are they related to his being a Knower? I mean, do you ever wish you had a normal relationship?"

"Everyday," Vivian answered quickly, but seeing Alex's frown, she laughed and then elaborated. "I'd love to be able to tell him a little white lie, if I thought it'd make him stress less. I'd love to be able to make love and exchange essence as often as we wanted without having flashes of his gift startle me—which both annoys him, because, as you know, he hates it when the tables are turned, but also worries him, because even after all this time, he fears I'll get tired of it and ask him to leave. Heck, I'd love to be able to tell him a joke without him plucking the punch line from my head before I reach the end. But all of that is because I love the big lug nut. If I ever wish Sage were normal, or at least not gifted, it's because I see how difficult it is for him; I don't wish it for my own sake."

Alex nodded, not entirely convinced, but appreciative that Vivian tried.

"And don't give me that crap about you also being human and therefore even less accepted by the coven. Whether you give him credit for it or not, Markus feels the same way I do. Those who take issue with your being human or a Seer are the same vampires who won't look Sage in the eye when they talk to him. They're cowards who hide behind traditions and ideas of what's normal, because they're afraid of your power and aren't comfortable knowing the coven needs you."

"I thought Sage was the Knower," Alex chuckled.

"Well, Sage isn't as good as Markus at keeping others' secrets, not from me anyways. Little good it did you, though. He's more than willing to gripe about having to hear your constant worries, but wouldn't let me do anything to help. I told him and Markus months ago that having a chance to meet me and Cormelia would be good for you. But they both waited until—" Vivian cut herself off.

"Until I slit my wrist, had to feed from your mate, and nearly lost my own when he learned I'd kept it from him?" No one else was holding back tonight, why should Alex? "I'm not sure it would have been enough to prevent the first two, but some additional advice on the third would have been nice. I took too long to listen to the advice given to me by the one female in the coven I knew." Alex smiled at Sarah. Then she realized she never considered Vivian's role in that incident.

"Were you mad when he fed me?"

"It saved your life. I would have killed him if he hadn't. As the partner of a warrior, that kind of feeding to save another coven member is expected. I was a little pissed at you and Markus when I heard how you each treated him after, until he calmed down enough to admit that Markus didn't know the truth, and that you lost control because you were terrified he'd find out. Then I just felt bad for Markus. What you did, keeping the truth from him to 'protect' him, was the same thing Sage had done to every female he fed from. As I told him, as Cormelia told you earlier this evening, others have a right to decide for themselves what they can handle."

Alex should have known Vivian's brand of honesty would have a bite. She was Sage's partner, after all, and maybe they weren't quite as different as Alex had previously presumed.

Ellie honed in on another topic. "Is that why you two never mated? Because you like your independence?"

Alex thought she knew the answer to this question, which is why *sh*e never would have asked it. Vivian's mood and tone confirmed it.

"No. We've never mated because Sage is an even slower learner than Alex is with that particular lesson."

"Sorry. I just thought...never mind."

Cormelia shot Vivian, who was still stewing in her own thoughts, a scathing look before reaching out to Ellie. Alex didn't think it possible, but the redhead appeared to be blushing.

"Don't apologize, Ellie. Vivian's just a little rawer than usual on this topic lately."

"Why lately?" Ellie asked.

Cormelia looked to her roommate who tossed her hand aside, giving her permission to answer on her behalf.

"Alex and Markus's recent mating."

Alex tried to catch Vivian's eye, but the small vampire was glaring into the fire.

"Good to know that caused others problems."

"What?" Alex spun on Ellie. She could understand Sage and Vivian being affected. That she and Markus could mate, live under the same roof, and deal with the disapproval of Markus's family and coven proved that the same was true of the Knower and his long-time partner. What that had to do with Rocky and Ellie, though, she couldn't fathom.

"Rocky's been in a rush to mate ever since. If he could have afforded a ring and an apartment, he'd have had Darian preside over our mating ceremony the next night."

On second thought, that sounded like Rocky. He did nothing half-assed. If he loved Ellie, as Alex knew he deeply did, it fit that he'd be chomping at the bit.

"So what's the problem? I mean, outside of him being a released felon and you being a princess."

Ellie looked at her incredulously. Alex knew those were pretty huge hurdles, but considering the hurdles Ellie had been willing to jump to stay with Rocky, she expected the female to put up more of a fight. Unless…

"You don't want to mate him." Alex felt her chest tighten. She didn't know if it was the sensation of her heart breaking for her best friend or the building rage she felt towards Elizabeth.

"No. That's not it, Alex, and don't you dare tell him I said that. I just…want a little time. I risked everything to come here. And I risked it again to stay with Rocky." When Alex tried to butt in, reminding her that he'd risked the same for her, Ellie spat, "I know that much better than you do. And I don't regret any of it, even after what happened. I just think we both should enjoy our independence from our old lives awhile, before we create a new dependence."

"Unless you plan on dating other people, or vampires," Alex corrected, "you won't be anymore inhibited or dependent on him than you are now." The way Alex saw it, once one went as far as committing to be someone's feeding partner, a mating ceremony was a mere formality.

"Did anyone explain to her the meaning of her mating vows?" Ellie addressed Sarah, obviously taking a different stance on coven ceremonies. "Wasn't your own mate beaten because of something *you* did? Rocky spent two years walking on eggshells, terrified that I'd do something to expose myself—and my relationship with him. It's bad enough he still has to worry about his own decisions as a newly freed male whom half the coven would love to see mess up. I don't want him to worry about my mistakes, too. And I don't want to have to think about his reputation being tarnished every time I make a decision."

"I understand," Alex nodded. "You're saying you learned nothing from me or Sage." It was catty but true.

"What I heard was that she wants the freedom you and Sage both had to learn things on her own." Sarah shot Alex a look that should have kept her quiet.

"Fine, she's free to repeat mistakes from history as often as she chooses, but if she breaks his heart again—"

"Whose fault was it that I nearly broke his heart the first time?"

"The Vengatti's," Vivian cut in before the argument escalated. "And the traitor's. He gave the information to the Vengatti, and they decided what to do with it. I'm sure Alex will cop to some poor decision making surrounding that, but laying the blame on her is too much, Ellie." Vivian said no more. Ellie didn't argue, except, of course, with Alex.

"I was his friend and partner well before you stumbled into his life. I know a thing or two about his heart, even more than you, Seer."

Alex wondered if Ellie knew exactly how close to the mark she was with her first comment. It was a miracle Sage and Rocky had been there to rescue her the night the Vengatti first tried to snatch her. Alex had literally stumbled into Rocky's arms. Of course, not knowing he was there to help, she had kicked him in the groin, a move she repeated the next day when he stopped her from running away. That they developed a friendship at all was a stroke of luck, very good luck, in Alex's opinion. She wondered if Ellie had shared a taste of that same luck, when she first arrived in Bristol, stumbling into Rocky, the one Rectinatti as in need of blood and secrecy as she.

"I believe you," Alex told her in a softer tone. "And I'm guessing you're even more appreciative than I am for having found him."

"Does a Seer really have to guess when it comes to emotions?" Vivian asked lightly.

Alex grinned. "Not really, but sometimes we have to bring up a topic in order to be sure."

Ellie cracked a small smile. "Then you're sure now."

"Yup, but I still want to hear how it happened—how two lone vampires, in a city with far too many other vamps roaming around, managed to find each other without being discovered first."

Ellie's eyes darted to Sarah. Alex could sense she was worried that revealing too much would have further repercussions. Rocky's sentence was over, but explaining the extent he went to break it in order to find a feeding partner might still pose him a danger. Apparently, though, membership in the SVC came with some privileges.

"Darian already knows and dealt with the worst of it, Ellie," Sarah assured her. "Neither you nor Rocky have to worry about me telling him the rest, if you choose to tell us."

Ellie nodded, but then turned to Alex and Vivian. "And neither of you will breathe a word of it to Markus or Sage—even if parts of it will infuriate them?" Ellie understood that this could be a temptation rather than a deterrent, depending on the day. She watched warily as Vivian and Alex exchanged smiles.

"What infuriates Sage, usually entertains me," Vivian

admitted. "But I'll keep this one to myself. I promise."

Alex had the same sentiment when it came to Markus, but there was another hitch.

"Sage. I can't always block him. He wouldn't rat Rocky out, but I can't promise he won't abuse him as soon as my mate and Darian leave the house."

"I can," Vivian said. "If he ever wants to feed again. It's okay, Ellie, tell your tale. It's getting late, and I'd love to leave here without the taste of Henry still in my mouth." She made a face like she just bit into a lemon. Alex cracked up.

Sarah and Cormelia shared the same exasperated expressions they'd been exchanging all evening.

"Sorry, was that pun in poor taste? Is a century too soon to be cracking jokes about something that could have gotten me locked up for life?"

"I'm pretty sure, even without the time-lapse, your actions would be excused," Ellie assured her with a darkening expression. "I hope the same will be said for Rocky's when I'm through." She was eying Alex, the one female who hadn't been able to promise that her story wouldn't be repeated. There was another promise Alex could make her, though, one the other females couldn't.

Alex held her fist to her heart and bowed, the warriors' vow. "Nobody will hurt Rocky, Ellie. Not when I'm around. Not for anything you tell us, or for any other reason, for that matter. You may not particularly like me, but I love Rocky like a brother, and I've lost too many of those already."

Ellie's expression didn't change, but her emotions did. When she replied Alex sensed more appreciation and respect behind the words than anyone else could have deciphered from the actual response.

"I know that. And the fact that he feels the same way

toward you is just one reason I don't particularly like you. But I guess I do trust you, warrior, at least where Rocky's concerned."

Alex nodded, accepting that when it came to her relationship with Ellie, this might be the best she could hope for.

6. Blood and Secrecy:
Ellie & Rocky's Story

Bristol, Massachusetts, 2008

"Last call jerk alert," Talia muttered to Ellie motioning to the far end of the bar. With her hip she slammed the cash register drawer shut with unnecessary force. "He's all yours, because I swear if he orders anything more than a single bottle of beer, I'll rip his head off."

Talia took the two beers and one rum and coke she'd been fixing off the counter and spun on her heels to deliver them to the three already plastered underage drinkers awaiting them. Ellie laughed, and not just at Talia's peep-toe heels which were utterly impractical for a bartender working a seven-hour shift and a clear violation of the board of health's dress code for food and beverage servers. More amusing was the thirty-something's tough-as-nails attitude. The truth was, of the two bartenders working the Tuesday night crowd, only one of them had the capability to rip heads off, and it wasn't the one wearing too-tight jeans and a plum-lipped pout.

"What do you want?" Ellie called down to the end of the bar where the dark-haired newcomer stood biting at his thumbnail. He didn't look up from under his baseball hat. She figured he didn't hear her over the din of the small, but, by this point, very drunk groups of kids from the nearby college. She was about to ask again when she heard him answer.

"A beer…and a couple shots."

Ellie stopped wiping the counter mid-swipe to stare at him. Being new, she had more patience than Talia for the idiots who waited until ten minutes before last call to stroll in and try to down enough drinks to leave as drunk as their buddies. She was beginning to wonder, though, if her coworker and roommate had pegged this one right.

"You're going to have to be a little more specific." She waved her hand impatiently over the ten different taps and three-dozen bottles of liquor. With his hat as low over his eyes as it was, she wasn't even certain he saw.

He dug a crumpled bill out of his front pocket and flattened it on the bar.

"Whatever's cheap."

Talia snorted behind her. "Bet you my night's tips that ain't no twenty he plans on leaving you."

Ellie pulled down a beer glass and two shot glasses while scowling at her. Unlike Talia, her enhanced vision allowed her to confirm what she also would have suspected. "I'll bet you the thirty-seven cents left over after he pays for his Icehouse draft and two shots of gut-rot vodka with that ten, that he'll still be nursing them when we're trying to close up."

Talia tightened her dark ponytail, shaking her head. "You can keep the thirty-seven cents, honey. And if you can get rid of him before closing, I'll buy us both a drink before Joe locks up."

"Don't hold your sober breath," Ellie told her sliding the drinks down the sticky counter. She didn't bother to speak to him as she plucked the bill off the worn polyurethaned wood, so she supposed it wasn't fair to expect a thank you, but she did. When he remained silent, jaw-dropped, gawking at her like she was a piece of meat, she practically snarled.

"Asshole," she muttered spinning back to the register. It wasn't until she snapped the ten-dollar bill in front of Talia as evidence that she caught the scent.

She brought it to her nose to be sure, then whipped around so fast she realized it couldn't have looked human. Luckily Talia was too busy laughing at her to catch the movement.

"Are you sniffing that thing?" She snatched the bill from Ellie's frozen hands. "Do you know where that's been?"

Talia's eyes finally followed Ellie's to the end of the bar where two empty shot glasses and a drained beer glass were all that remained of the male who had just been there.

"Nice work. What'd you say to scare him off so fast?"

"I—I didn't." Ellie's heart was racing. She had known it was inevitable. That she'd made it nearly a week without running into another vampire in a city with a coven as large as Bristol's was unbelievable. She had just planned, or optimistically hoped anyways, that when she did, she'd have a chance to explain herself. But he was gone.

"Hey, you okay?" Talia was suddenly serious having seen the intensity of Ellie's reaction. "You look like you've seen a ghost—or maybe a blast from your past? Please tell me this doesn't smell like your old beau?" She was sniffing the bill with a crinkled nose.

Ellie collected herself and jumped on Talia's words. She pretended to blush in embarrassment. "I thought I caught a whiff of his cologne, that's all. It just…surprised me." If she had meant any of it, she would have been embarrassed. Fleeing the West Coast over a bad break-up had been a lame story, but Talia had bought it easily the first night Ellie showed up at the bar asking about work. Talia had done her one better by offering up her futon as well.

"Honey, you've got it worse than I thought. You're all the way across the country. Time to move on. Although if you decide to stay in Bristol, you'll find the pickings slim. We might need to make a girls' night trip into Boston one of our nights off. We can pick up some young, rich Harvard boys."

Ellie smiled. Talia didn't need to know that Ellie's family would make most of those Harvard boys look mundanely middle-class.

"Thanks, Talia, for everything."

Talia winked and returned to cleaning up the last of the night's empties.

Forty minutes later the lights were on illuminating the stale beer stains on the painted concrete floor and signaling to the last of the lingerers that it was time to leave. Joe, the bouncer and part owner, shooed the final crew though the door while Ellie counted out her tips and closed down the register.

"Leave it," he said when she had bent over to pick up the last bin of dirty glasses to be brought back to the dishwasher. "Talia and I'll lock up. You go home."

Ellie looked back at Talia with one brow raised. Her new roommate wore the kind of smile that said, 'don't wait up.' Ellie had spent her first twenty-six years up all night, but she got the message.

"Okay, then." She grabbed her purse from under the bar and headed to the door Joe held open for her. She slapped the cash pouch into his chest on the way out. "Be safe." She winked at him.

He whacked her ass with the pouch as he shut the door behind her. "Watch it, new girl."

She flipped him the bird before tugging her light winter jacket closed against the cold late February wind.

Once the door had latched, sealing behind her the smell of body odor, sweet mixers, and spilled booze, she inhaled deeply. If Talia and Joe hadn't started in yet on their extra-curricular activities and happened to glance through the pane of glass on the door, it'd simply look like she was breathing in the fresh air. Ellie had another motive. Sure enough, she caught the scent. It was mingled with a dozen other human scents, but there was no mistaking the smell of another Rectinatti vampire in the mix.

Half of her wanted to bolt in the opposite direction, to go a block out of her way just to avoid him. The other half of her knew that was pointless. He had either fled to report her instantly to the coven's warriors, and was therefore long gone. Or he had waited, planning to question her himself, in which case he was somewhere right outside the bar, where he could see her leave. Or if he tracked her scent, the way she now tracked his, he was waiting on the doorstep of the apartment she'd been sharing with Talia for less than a week. Ellie was fairly certain Talia wouldn't slip in before dawn. She also believed another Rectinatti wouldn't intentionally harm her or her roommate. Still, it wasn't a chance she wanted to take. She turned in the direction of the scent.

A hundred yards later, when the hand reached out of the shadows to tug her coat sleeve, Ellie was ready. With a twist of her wrist, it was she holding him. She yanked his arm up behind him and slammed his chest against the side of the alley between the bar and row of shops next to it. He grunted but didn't move to stop her—until she jammed a hand into the waistband of his baggy jeans.

"Whoa, stop! Put that down before you hurt yourself. It's not a toy." The stocky male had spun around and stood facing the barrel of his own gun. He held one open hand up by his shoulder in a sign of surrender. The other he reached out to her, expecting she'd return his weapon to it.

Ellie couldn't help but be reminded of her father's warriors back home, always treating her like a little princess capable of nothing more than dressing up dolls. Thankfully, her father had wanted a boy, an heir, and was more than happy to let Ellie train and play with the warriors' sons, at least until he had one of his own.

She deftly ejected the magazine, confirmed the caliber of ammunition he was using, and then snapped it back into place.

"Forty-fives. Hollow points, I bet. No, I guess you're right. This one's not a toy. Although those do seem like overkill to scare off the punks you'll find hanging around here after hours. Unless you had tougher targets in mind?"

"I wasn't...How do you...Just give me back the gun. I'm not here to hurt you." He dropped both hands by his sides.

"Sending a hulking armed male in a dark hoody to jump out of an alley is an odd form of welcome. Is that coven tradition?"

"You *are* from another coven then. Portland or Vancouver?"

"Vancouver is an eclectic group of strays, with no

Regan. I'd hardly qualify that as a coven." Ellie turned the Beretta around to carefully hand back to him. He took it, grinning at her.

"West Coast, then, Portland. Did you get lost on your way back to Ireland, or were you spying for Jamison to report back how a real coven works?"

Ellie blanched at the mention of her father, the Regan of the West Coast coven. When the male rushed to apologize after seeing her reaction, she realized he hadn't said it because he recognized her. It was just his poor attempt at humor.

"Hey, I'm kidding. I'm not accusing you of anything. I just…" His words trailed off.

Ellie wasn't the only one acting nervous. He was tapping his fingers on his thigh. She detected the faint smell of blood and saw two of his nails were bitten to the quick.

"Who are you?"

"Me?" He looked up in surprise. He clearly didn't like their roles being reversed. "I'm…nobody."

"How Emily Dickenson of you."

"Huh?"

It was sadly comforting to know the males on the East Coast were as uncultured as those on the West.

"What does the depressed poet chick have to do with anything?"

I take that back, she thought. He wasn't uncultured, just sexist. Although she admitted she was a little impressed he knew the poet, she wasn't going to waste her breath reciting the poem. She just wanted a chance to explain herself.

"I was asking your name. For instance, mine's Ellie." This was only a half-truth, Ellie being the cover name she had been using since running away. But she wasn't about to explain that either.

The male sneered at her condescending tone, but answered. "I'm Sl—Rocky."

"You sure?" He clearly was making up some bullshit name mid-reply.

"Yeah, I'm sure," he snapped. "What I'm not sure about is what the hell I'm still doing here."

"You're the one who pulled me in here. Why?" Ellie played it cool, putting it all back on him, though it was she who had the most to lose.

Rocky deliberated before responding.

"I thought maybe you needed help."

Ellie considered telling him he thought wrong or that she didn't play the damsel in distress role very well. But the truth was she did need help. Or she would very soon. Without a feeding partner, she'd have to scurry back to her father with her tail between her legs.

"What kind of help?"

Rocky grinned. "The same kind I need, an exchange of sorts."

It couldn't be that easy. A Rectinatti male happens to show up at her work looking for a feeding partner. This had her father written all over it.

"Fine. Give me your wrist." She hoped to call his bluff.

"Um, okay." The dark-haired male seemed baffled but slid up the sleeve on his right arm and held it out to her, stepping close enough that it nearly touched her lips.

She shoved him back into the wall. He looked as confused as she felt.

"Are you serious? Do you really not know who I am?"

"You're Ellie, small arms aficionado and American poet lover from Portland. Is there something else I need to know?" He was back to nervously tapping his nails on his leg.

Ellie laughed as relief swept over her. He was serious; he had no idea who she was.

"I don't get it, though. Why are you willing to do this?"

"To feed you? I told you; I need it as much as you do."

"But you understand I'm here illegally and that I have no intention of announcing myself to your Regan?"

His tapping increased. "That's not the smartest decision, but it's yours to make, I suppose."

"Damn right," was her knee-jerk response.

Rocky nodded. "You're obviously here for a reason." He looked around at the garbage-filled alleyway and sighed. "So am I. You need help if you're going to stay here. I need help if I'm…I just need help. I won't ask questions, if you won't. And I certainly won't tell anyone, if you do me the same favor."

"So you'll show up once a week, exchange essence, and leave? How romantic." It was actually perfect, but Ellie wasn't about to let on to that just yet.

Rocky was scuffing his boot on the filthy snow. "It's kind of the best I can offer right now. If you find a real partner and want to stop, we will. I'll still keep your secret."

Ellie couldn't believe she was about to agree to this. Feeding from a male she hardly knew, a male who admittedly wanted her for nothing more than her essence, made her feel cheap. Looking at Rocky with his gnawed nails and nervous shuffling, though, she considered that he might have been feeling the same way.

"Okay. Where do you want to go?"

Rocky sighed in relief, but then the pained look

returned. "I don't have much time tonight. Any night, really."

"Do you have a car nearby?"

"No!" He practically shouted it at her. "I mean, I do, but you can't be in it. It's a loaner, and your scent will be hard to explain to…my boss."

"Well, I live halfway across the city." Ellie sighed looking at the snow-covered filth in which they were standing. She reluctantly pulled up her sleeve. "I'll do it here tonight, but from now on you get to the bar earlier so we can use the backroom or the employee's bathroom." Neither was luxurious or even particularly clean, but just about anywhere had to be a step up from where they currently stood, surrounded by trash and the sickening effluvium of human urine.

How far the princess had fallen.

"Sure. Thanks." His own sleeve was still rolled from earlier.

It took them a minute of awkward shifting to find a position from which each could drink. They ended in a loose embrace with their free hands on the other's lower back.

Rocky released his fangs and bit greedily into her veins. He seemed desperate for it as soon as her wrist was under his nose. She guessed he was a few years younger than she, and therefore naturally had a stronger need. She wondered how one so young had no partner, no family or friend to feed from. She almost wished she hadn't agreed not to ask.

Finally she bit into him and began to draw essence. It was easy. He was pure, strong. It surprised her. He tasted sweet, but there was an edge to him that her feeding partner back home never had. It was something she would have asked her grandmother about, had she been able. The ancient female had always had more patience for her granddaughter's endless questions, boundless energy, and strength, all of which, according to Ellie's mother, was more befitting a male. Ellie and her grandmother had shared everything until the day Ellie decided to leave that life behind. With a twinge of regret, she withdrew and licked the wound clean.

Feeling her mouth leave his wrist, Rocky pulled back, too, gently stopping her blood with his venom.

"I'm sorry. I didn't realize how thirsty I was. Are you okay?"

"I'm fine," Ellie replied curtly.

"Oh. I just thought...at the end, that you were upset."

"You tasted that?"

Rocky shrugged. "I guess."

The older females liked to tell tales, one of which was that only one fated to be your mate could taste such nuances in your blood. For a moment it made her even more curious about what she tasted in his. She ran her tongue pensively over her lip, until she realized he was watching.

Creator, what was wrong with her tonight? The thought had obviously surfaced because she'd been thinking about her gram. She shook it firmly from her mind.

"It was nothing, but thanks for asking." She rolled down her sleeve, buttoned the cuff, and headed back onto the main sidewalk.

Rocky flashed to her side. "Want me to wait with you while you call a cab?"

"I walk."

"By yourself? In the middle of the night? Halfway across town? There are Vengatti in Portland, right? That was why some of the coven from Ireland settled there, wasn't it? Because there are plenty of them here, Ellie, and they don't just hunt humans."

It took a Herculean effort not to roll her eyes at his condescending comments. If he knew how well versed she was, not only in both covens' histories, but also in the atrocities of the Vengatti, he would know she didn't need this lecture.

"I did my homework, and I take precautions. You're not the only one who comes prepared." Ellie shook her hand inside her coat pocket, already gripping the handle of a knife.

Rocky looked impressed for a total of three seconds. "Still, I don't like it." His expression was pained as she shrugged and made to leave. He held out a hand to stop her while reaching into his pant's pocket. He pulled out a watch, apparently checking to see if he had time to escort her. She would have laughed at the tough looking vamp in destroyed-style designer jeans carrying an old-school pocket watch, but when he snapped closed the cover, she froze. The ornate R marked the piece as a coven heirloom, rare and valuable enough that only a handful of coven families could have afforded it. Even fewer would be allowed to possess it. He saw the cold rage boiling up in her expression as he slid it back into his pocket.

"It was a gift. I can explain—"

"How a member of a first family can't afford to leave a bartender a tip? Or why he's pretending he needs essence from random rogue vampires he happens to meet in college bars? If you're here to bring me home or to report me to your Regan, you had no right to drink from me." Her slap knocked his head to one side and left her hand stinging. She spun on her heals, flashing down the nearest side street.

He caught up to her midway down the block, nearly

tackling her onto the icy pavement. He threw out one hand to catch them both. The other he had wrapped around her to keep her from hitting the ground. He didn't let go as he pulled her to her feet. So she was right. He was here to take her, to whom she didn't know or care. It meant the same. She was heading back to a life she hated.

She wondered how many human girls grew up wishing they could be exotic princesses, with wealth, strength, and status. The same number, she supposed, who had no idea what it was like to have your every move scrutinized, to have status but no power or freedoms, to have to watch, wearing a pretty face and elegant gowns, as those younger and less wise than you were trained to do a job that would have been yours, if only you had been born a prince instead. Would any of them believe it possible to wish to be a bartender in a dive, with hardly enough money to buy groceries, never mind gowns?

She looked up at her captor, only to find his dark eyes as dejected as she imagined her own looked.

"I'm not pretending. I'm not here to bring you anywhere. And I'm not a part of a first family—not anymore." The last two words seemed to stick in his throat. He released her, then reached up to smooth her collar, which had been tugged astray in their fall. The simple gesture struck her more than his next words. "I really did just 'happen' upon you tonight, even if that sounds like something an elder would say. And I was really lucky and really happy I did."

"Was?" Ellie's voice sounded small. She couldn't fathom how his story could be true. The pieces seemed too random, but perhaps if they were shaken out in the right light, they'd fall together.

Rocky chuckled, but there was a hint of hysteria to it as he looked at the new cuts in his palm from breaking their fall. "I wasn't supposed to be here tonight, so unless I think of a way of explaining this, and this," he touched the red welt left by her hand, "I'm pretty sure I won't be back next week. Or ever."

Ellie's concern grew. His fear was as genuine as his intentions had been. If she hadn't so grossly misjudged that moments ago, he'd have no reason for his hands to be shaking as they were.

"Fall on it."

"What?"

"Turn your head. I'll hold your hands so you don't instinctively break the fall again." She gently turned his head so her handprint faced forward. "All of Bristol is one big ice puddle this week. Wherever you were supposed to be tonight surely has ice you could have slipped on, yes?"

Rocky nodded. "Do it."

She grabbed his hands and used her foot to kick his legs out from under him, sending him face first onto the pavement.

He let out a tirade of curses that lasted a full minute and would have curled her mother's toes. She knelt next to him as he finally pushed himself to his knees.

"Oh, shit. I am so sorry." She slapped her hand over her mouth, startled by her own response to seeing his scratched and bruised cheek.

Rocky managed to grin at her cursing. "Just tell me it hides the hand print, so we don't have to do that again."

Ellie tilted his head towards the nearest streetlight to be sure. "You're good. Too good. I really am sorry—for everything."

"It's okay." Rocky got to his feet and brushed off the front of his sweatshirt. "I do need to go, though." He was looking at his boots.

"Then go. Don't be late. I'll get home safely, I promise. And maybe next week you can tell me how one manages to get free from a first family." Ellie threw in the last line nervously, unsure if their arrangement still stood.

"Maybe. Maybe you can tell me how a female knows how to handle a Beretta and execute a sweep kick better than most warriors."

Ellie smiled. "Maybe."

She turned around and continued walking down the street. She was sure he watched her go, but she didn't bother to look back as she waved goodbye over her shoulder.

Ellie was glad Talia and Joe's on-again-off-again relationship had been going steady since last week. Otherwise she was certain Talia would have noticed her constantly checking the door with each new group of drinkers who entered. Instead she was spending as much time as possible sashaying her bare midriff by the table in the back of the bar where Joe sat.

Ellie mentally slapped herself. It was only an hour after sunset. Rocky had made it clear it wasn't easy for him to come and go from wherever he was staying without questions being asked. Maybe he wasn't going to show up at all. Because he couldn't, or because he didn't want to. And would that bother her? Feeding from him last week bought her more time. That was what mattered.

Yet when she caught sight of him entering the bar a little after ten, she couldn't help but smile, an expression she quickly wiped off her face before he looked up and saw it. He appeared more at ease this week. After a quick surveillance of the crowd, he swiped off his hat and shoved it in his back pocket as he mussed his thick dark hair with his other hand. Ellie looked away as he turned in her direction. He'd have to come to her.

"Hey," he said as he pushed his way up to the bar.

"Oh, hi. You made it back, I see. I'm guessing that means they bought the excuse last week." Ellie didn't even know who 'they' were, but it was an easy conversation starter, even if it did give away that she had worried about him.

He ground his teeth. "Yeah, it worked—too well. In addition to thinking I'm a thug, they now think I'm also the world's klutziest—" He cut himself off realizing how close he was to half a dozen humans.

Seeing his cheeks flush, Ellie laughed. "How about a drink?"

He shook his head, his blush deepening. She figured the reason for it and grabbed a bottle of their best Irish whiskey, which she was sure her father would still consider cheap crap. She filled a tumbler well past what a double shot would be.

"On the house."

Rocky looked torn about accepting it. She realized she probably punctured his male pride but intended to keep the whiskey flowing long enough that he wouldn't care.

"Really, no one in this crowd ever orders it anyway."

He shrugged and downed it in a single swig.

"There's a reason for that." He coughed, yet allowed her to refill the glass. "Anyone under three hundred hasn't lived long enough to acquire a taste for this shit." He threw back the second glassful as fast as the first.

She put a finger to her lips to remind him to keep the vampire references to a minimum, as she filled his glass again.

"Nurse that one a little. I've got other paying customers I've got to get hammered." She winked and headed back to the other end of the bar.

A little after midnight Ellie was becoming impatient. The crowd wasn't thinning, and Talia was still spending more time on Joe's lap than serving drinks. Finally she returned to fill a few orders, and Ellie snagged her.

"Hey, I'm taking a fifteen in the back. Watch the bar for me."

Talia bristled, a little surprised at Ellie's command, but eventually nodded. Ellie thanked her before sliding out the small opening in the counter and heading to the hallway leading to the back room. She waited until she could hear Talia taking orders before turning around to motion to Rocky. There was no need. He was already on her heels, causing her to startle.

"Sorry. I just figured you wanted me to follow."

Ellie shushed him and pushed him along in front of her. Once in the back office, which also served as a break room on the rare occasion one of them got a break, Ellie shut and locked the door.

"You could've waited a few minutes, so it wasn't so obvious." She turned around to face the room.

"Why bother? Humans are oblivious." He was right behind her again, already rolling up his sleeve. Seeing how eagerly he positioned himself next to her, she began to wonder if he *couldn't* have waited.

"How old are you?" She tried to determine the reason behind his desire.

"Old enough that I shouldn't need essence this badly so soon."

Ellie began to smile, until he continued.

"I started a new job with the warriors, which requires some physical training, and I guess I'm still recovering from…anyways, I'm sorry if I'm a little too eager."

Her jaw set. It wasn't what she expected, although she didn't understand why this more practical answer offended her.

"It's fine. Take what you need." She unceremoniously shoved her wrist in his face. He hesitated for a moment watching her expression, but his need conquered his curiosity. He sank his fangs into her flesh and drank greedily.

Pissed, for no apparent reason other than that she hadn't been the cause of his desire, she tore into his skin harder than she ought to. Instead of the gasp she expected, Rocky moaned.

That's better.

When he finally lapped the marks on her wrist and stepped back, Ellie saw further evidence that her essence wasn't the only thing Rocky enjoyed, or wanted to. Despite the baggy jeans, it was clear she had other appeal to the male vamp. He noticed her looking and grinned sheepishly.

"Sorry," he mumbled.

"For being attracted to me?"

"For not having the control to hide it."

Ellie shrugged. "Guess that's another benefit of being female."

With a smug grin she flipped the lock on the door and headed into the hall. She heard him stumble over his own feet as he tried to pursue her.

"Wait. Does that mean—"

A cacophony of angry voices coming from the hall cut him off.

"You touch me again, and I'll rearrange your face, creep!"

"Come on, your ass is asking to be slapped in a skirt like that."

Ellie rolled her eyes at the two drunks and their posses of friends going at it. In the two short weeks she'd worked there, she'd already become immune to such scenes. Rocky, however, couldn't seem to stop watching as the two groups volleyed slurred insults back and forth. When one of the boys reached out and twisted the wrist of a girl who'd just thrown a drink in his face, Ellie saw Rocky stiffen.

"Joe's got it. Don't worry about it."

The girl tried to slap her captor, but he easily grabbed her other hand and yanked her into him.

Something in Rocky snapped. His fangs sprang. Ellie saw his hand plunge into the pocket of his hoody, where she was sure he kept a knife. She yanked him back by the hood, pinning him to the wall in the darkened hallway from which they had been emerging.

"Calm down! People will see!"

Rocky released a snarl and struggled against her. Worried one of the bar goers would turn and catch a glimpse of his fangs, and terrified he was out of control enough to use them, Ellie did the only thing she could to cover them. She pressed her body to his, holding his wrists with all her strength. She smothered his mouth with her own, kissing him violently between the words she hissed at him too fast for any human to comprehend.

"Get control of yourself, now...you'll expose us both...retract your fangs, Rocky." She glanced over her shoulder. "It's all over...the girl's okay."

At that, the switch flipped again. Rocky retracted his fangs. He looked across the bar to where Joe and another bouncer had split up the brawl. Then his eyes rested on Ellie. She was still practically touching her lips to his.

"Fuck." His eyes were wide, his breath shallow gasps; he clearly realized how close he had come to losing it. "I'm so sorry." He tried to push away.

"No. It's okay." She leaned in to kiss him again,

gently, soothingly. She wasn't pretending this time. He had only wanted to help the girl, a human he didn't even know. His reaction had been stupid, dangerous even. It was also a turn on.

Rocky began kissing her back as intensely as he had fed from her. As close to him as she was, she could feel his erection return. This time it didn't fill her with smug satisfaction, but another more intense emotion. Wrapping one leg around his, she was able to press herself against him, but grinding through their thick winter clothes did little to satisfy her desire. It only intensified her urgings until she ached.

"Hey, Ginger, when you're done dry-humping the customers, would you mind returning to the bar?" Joe nudged his elbow into her back as he walked past carrying a crate of dirty glasses into the kitchen.

Rocky's snarl returned, but luckily Joe hadn't looked back after making the rude, but accurate remark. Ellie unentwined herself and stepped back to catch her breath. Finally, she and Rocky snapped back to reality where they stood in plain sight of a few dozen humans. There was a moment of awkward silence.

"I've got to get back. You, um, you ought to go."

"No." Rocky shook his head. "I've got more time tonight. I wanted to walk you home."

Ellie smiled as she ran a hand down his chest. "I know what you want, Rocky. It's not going to happen. Not tonight."

Rocky sneered, tugging his sweatshirt down. "That's not what I was talking about. I told you last week, I don't like you walking home by yourself."

"And I told you last week, that I can handle myself. And here I am, safe and sound, as promised."

He sighed heavily.

"Maybe next week. You still owe me a story, remember?"

His grimace shifted into a grin. "You owe me one in return, if I remember correctly."

"And if you're a good male and go home like I'm asking you to, you just might hear it—eventually."

"You sure you're not from a first family, too?"

Ellie blanched momentarily, hoping he couldn't see it in the poor lighting. She'd been away from other vampires too long, though, if she believed that'd work.

"Why?" She tried sounding cavalier.

His grin grew. He didn't buy it. "Because you seem awfully comfortable giving orders and expecting to get your way."

Ellie flipped her long red hair over her shoulders as if she were annoyed with him and headed back to the bar. Before he could stop her to apologize, or badger her, or whatever he hoped to do, she waved him off without looking back.

"'Night, Rocky. See you next week."

Once behind the bar she looked up to see if he was still there. Her eyes scanned the crowd, which had thinned since the fight, and found him gone. She smiled. Yes, she did indeed like getting her way.

Later that night, back at the flat she shared with Talia, it occurred to her that Rocky, as a first family son himself, might have liked it just as much. As she went to pull the shades so she could slip off her grimy work clothes, she was nearly certain she spied Rocky pulling away from the curb half a block away in a white pick-up truck with its lights off. Recalling her reaction to his similar heroics back at the bar, her scowl softened. She didn't want to be anybody's damsel in distress, but watching her knight in shining armor ride off on his white steed really was kind of hot.

Exactly a week later Rocky swaggered into Mad Murphy's like he owned the place. He eased his way to the bar, nudging a few humans aside with his thick shoulders.

"Where's Ellie?" he demanded of Talia as soon as she was in earshot.

"She took the night off." Talia waited until his shoulders slumped before leaning over the bar in front of him. Her hot pink lace bra peeked over the top of her thin white v-neck tank. "Anything *I* can get you?"

Rocky gave her one revolted look before turning around.

"Right answer." Ellie had sneaked up behind him. She stood blocking his path wearing a wicked grin. "Thanks, Talia. See you later?"

"Maybe." Her roommate glanced over at Joe who was entertaining some jailbait in the corner. Winter break for Bristol's two high schools meant the fake IDs were worse than usual, and Talia's jealousy had left her pissy and miserable since last Friday. Ellie was glad to get a night away.

"C'mon. Let's get out of here." As she weaved her way outside, she grabbed Rocky's hand, a gesture that seemed to please him based on the dumb grin he suddenly wore. *Sweet*, she told herself, *not dumb*.

"Was that a test?" he asked as soon as they were clear of the rowdy crowd.

Ellie shrugged. She continued down the main road side-stepping the dirty snow piles.

"Where are we going? Your apartment's in the other direction."

She spun on him. He cringed, obviously aware he'd

been caught.

"Did you park there tonight? So you could spy on me again?"

"I won't have to spy, if you invite me over. We could pick up where we left off last week." His smug grin was evidence of his newfound boldness.

"You mean when I attacked you with my mouth to keep you from going Vengatti on some drunken college kids?"

"Is that how you remember it? Because I recall some beautiful redhead initiating round two after that little scene had ended." With a salacious grin he tried to pull her body against his. She yanked her hand free.

"I think your coven's Knower must have messed with your memories since last week. This redhead requires better foreplay than being snarled at. Perhaps a nice dinner, a bottle of wine?"

His grin was gutted. He began chipping at an icy snow bank with the toe of his heavy black boot. The comment had been a low blow; he had made it clear last week money was an issue. She was just letting him know he'd have to work a little harder.

"It's on me, and no macho arguments. As you correctly guessed last week, I can afford it—at least until my stash runs out."

Rocky looked up. Her plan had worked. Divulging this little detail had diverted his focus from his ego to his curiosity.

"So you are from a first family."

Ellie only smiled. It wouldn't have been lying to tell him yes. A Regan's family is technically a first family, especially in her father's case. Her grandfather had only been a member of the Elder Council when the coven moved from Ireland and a small group split for the West

Coast. Unlike the Bristol coven Regan, who'd been born into a long line of Regans, her grandfather had been chosen by the other Elders who settled in the Portland area, to serve as the small new coven's leader. Still, she couldn't bring herself to purposely deceive Rocky. She wasn't willing to risk his safety or hers by being forthcoming, but she could at least make it clear she was withholding information. She hoped that degree of honesty would suffice.

He nodded. His knit brows told her he knew there was something to her silence, but, for now, at least, he refrained from asking.

Two hours later when they were leaving a Japanese restaurant a few blocks from the bar, his questions started up again.

"Now that had to be a test. You watch Fear Factor too much growing up?"

Rocky's tone was sour, but Ellie ignored it. She knew it had nothing to do with the raw fish she had forced him to try. After a few sakes and a lesson in mixing the wasabi into the soy sauce, Rocky had enjoyed the meal. And they both enjoyed the company. He was just miffed she had chosen someplace on the pricey side and then insisted on paying for it. Or, more to the point, she guessed, he was humiliated that he wouldn't have had the money to split the bill if she had asked. Although he had chatted easily through dinner, he hadn't volunteered why that was so, even with his new job. She hadn't asked. It seemed fair. She had questions of her own that she didn't want to answer.

"Never really been a fan of television. Never had much time for it, really. But I love theater." This was something easy she could offer him.

"Like musicals?"

Ellie laughed. She'd heard elders talk about plagues with less distaste.

"I take it I shouldn't pick you up a ticket to the next Sondheim that comes to Bristol?"

"Nothing ever comes to Bristol. And if I'm going to risk going into Boston with you, it better be for something more exciting than a bunch of human dudes in tights."

"That'd be ballet, not theater. I'll cross out *The Nutcracker*, too."

Rocky stopped and squeezed her hand. He had taken it without comment as they left the restaurant. Pleased, she hadn't mentioned it.

"You think you'll still be around next December?"

"Hope so."

He nodded, then averted his eyes. "You think you'll still be feeding from a chump like me?"

She smiled, though he couldn't see it. They had more in common than either of them was willing to admit. One of her only friends back home had once accused Ellie of slipping into princess-mode anytime things got rough, feigning haughty detachment so everyone would keep their distance. It was her emotional safe haven. The friend had been right, of course, just as Ellie was right about Rocky. Humor was his harbor.

"No one's fooled by the one-liners or the self-deprecating jokes, you know."

Rocky looked up, searching for her real answer in her expression. She was about to end his agony when they heard the commotion.

Out of the corner of her eyes she saw the streaks from across the street. Other vampires. Three of them. Ellie started to turn, but Rocky reacted faster. He clamped one hand over her mouth and the other around her waist as he dragged her deep into the nearest alley between two three-storied apartment buildings. He pulled her up against the brick wall behind a large dumpster so neither could be seen from the street.

"Shh. I'll handle it. Stay here." He reached into her pocket and pulled out the knife she concealed there. "Anyone comes around this corner, stab them. I'll call out before I return."

Ellie started to protest, when a shriek of agony shattered the clear quiet, changing everything. She understood Rocky's intense gaze as they both peered over the dumpster toward the alley across from them. Two of the figures she had caught glimpses of were Vengatti. From the sound of it, the third, their intended victim, was a young Rectinatti male, one of Rocky's coven members, whom as a warrior, Rocky was sworn to protect.

"I promise. Go. Help him."

Rocky flashed back to the mouth of the alley, gun in hand. Ellie wanted to cry out to stop him, but she feared endangering everyone involved. He was new to his job, but he had to know using a gun in a close combat fight was insane.

Just then the young boy got in a blow to one of his attackers. For a split second the action slowed enough to be seen by human eyes. The shot rang out. One of the Vengatti hit the ground, the back of his skull blown out by the hollow point bullet. A fatal wound from nearly fifty yards, aimed at a moving vampire. Impossible.

Rocky turned, just long enough to motion her back out of sight, before stepping onto the sidewalk. Their position was obvious now. Ellie tightened her grip on the knife and listened. More shouts. There were at least two new voices. Rectinatti warriors, she prayed to the Creator.

Then footsteps coming too fast in her direction. No

one calling out to her. She thrust the knife forward into the chest of the large male who came around the corner. He spun in time to avoid the brunt of it.

"Rocky, what are you doing? You said you'd call out. They're still fighting." She stuck her head around the dumpster she'd been crouching behind, only to see the crowd in the alley had swelled to five. The young male, newly matured, at best, held one arm at an awkward angle, broken, no doubt. In his other hand he held a knife, which he slashed hesitantly when one of the Others got too close. The blurs, which she could hardly make out even with her enhanced vision, were two pairs of fighters, each comprised of a Vengatti male and an armed, trained Rectinatti warrior. Still she spun on Rocky. "The boy's injured and there was another Vengatti."

"He was in the alley. They were luring the kid there."

Ellie shuddered. Three grown males attacking a boy. They'd meant to drain him completely and leave behind the pile of ashes for his coven to find.

There was a grunt. Rocky peeked his head out again. When he pulled it back his look was one of agony. Only then did Ellie smell blood—Rocky's. She realized he might have had a reason not to return to the fight.

"Are you injured? Was it me? I thought I mostly missed." She pulled at the tear in the fabric of his dark hoody, trying to see the severity of his wound.

"It's just a flesh wound." He slapped her hand away with enough force to leave it stinging.

"Then go help them, warrior." She barked the command with a little too much ease. "I don't need a babysitter."

Rocky growled, spun, and slammed his fist into the brick wall sending crushed red stone cascading to the filthy ground. He had to have broken half the bones in his hand, but that wasn't the cause of his pained expression.

"I can't. I'm not a warrior. I only work for them." He was tugging at his dark hair, pacing the small hiding place.

Ellie was torn between sympathy, confusion, and...disgust.

"You're a male, aren't you?" If he had matured into a first family, as his pocket watch bearing the Rectinatti crest signified, he knew the coven's histories. He knew all males once served as warriors. He knew she was questioning his honor. She'd hoped it would spurn him into action. Instead he seemed to crumble. He slid down the brick wall and buried his face in one arm. When she saw him begin to tremble, she wanted to slap him. How could she have ever thought of him as her knight in shining armor?

"Your father disowned you, didn't he?" It all suddenly made sense. "Because you disgraced him. Because you refused to stand up for your own."

"Don't!" The word was a warning, a savage snarl.

When his head snapped up, it startled her further. His fangs were sprung, dripping with venom. His usually warm brown eyes bit into her with their blackness. The fist that wasn't broken was gripped like a vice around his knife. He hadn't been shaking with sobs, but with repressed rage. Rage that had boiled over at her accusation.

Ellie stepped back toward the chain link fence that separated the alley from the block behind it. If she had to, she could jump it.

Rocky reacted to something in her expression or her movement. His eyes widened and the knife clattered to the pavement. He fell forward from his crouch onto his knees.

"Ellie, I'm sorry. I can explain," he pleaded.

"Not now. The second Vengatti's dead, and the third just took off. They're not pursuing. They'll be here looking for the shooter any minute now. Let's go." She turned from him with the detachment she was infamous for and hopped the fence landing silently on the other side. She didn't ask what he was doing with the bag of trash he had pulled from the dumpster and was emptying in the alley. She didn't ask if he needed help maneuvering the fence with his injuries. She didn't care.

They stuck to the shadows moving silently through the neighborhoods that led to her and Talia's apartment. When she stepped out onto her block, she quickly surveyed the streets. Finding them empty, she turned to face him.

"Lift up your sweatshirt."

He hesitated, but when she reached for it, he helped hold it up out of the way of the wound.

"You should have stitches, but I suppose that would require too much explaining." She didn't wait for him to agree or disagree. She bent over and licked the cut closed as best she could. "If you have a first aid kit in that truck, I suggest wrapping it before you get to wherever you're going. And throw the sweatshirt out the window. You smell like blood and trash."

Rocky tried to speak, but she shoved her wrist to his mouth.

"Feed. You'll need it to heal the cut and your hand."

"Ellie, please." He pushed her hand away.

She didn't respond other than to tell him she'd need a little in exchange, since he'd be taking so much for his injuries.

"Ellie—"

"It's fine. You clearly need the essence more than I

do."

He flinched at this blow to his character.

Without waiting for him to offer it, she grabbed his injured hand, since the other still held his knife, and bit into his wrist. His essence tasted bitter tonight, hard to swallow. After a few mouthfuls, she pulled back, licking her fang marks. He drank another few deep pulls from her then did the same.

Ellie adjusted her sleeve and started across the street toward her stoop.

"Wait. Can I come up, to explain, please?"

"You need to go clean your gun and wash the residue from your hands. I can smell it from here."

Rocky squeezed his eyes shut in frustration. She doubted he knew his hand had gone to his pocket until it found nothing there. His expression changed instantly.

"The casing." His eyes darted back in the direction from which they had just fled. "I've got to go back."

Ellie swiped at his sleeve, holding him in place. "Are you kidding me? You wouldn't risk your ass to save that boy and two of your own warriors, but you'll risk going back to cover your tracks? I hoped I was wrong about what I said back there, but now I'm positive I was right. You're despicable."

She dropped his sleeve and started through the door.

"I wouldn't risk *your* ass earlier. Do you know how hard that was—to choose between everything I believe in, everything I want to be, and the female I—" He paused and swallowed back his anger along with whatever admission he had been about to make. "But you're right. There's no sense going back. It was your scent I covered with my own and with the trash. Mine's still there, casing or no casing."

Ellie froze with her hand on the knob. He *had* only

covered the back end of the alley, where she had hid, with the foul smelling garbage. She'd racked that up to him not wanting to be seen closer to the street.

"You're full of it. You could have sent me out the back and copped to any number of excuses for being there."

"No, I couldn't have, for a number of reasons, the least of which being that I live with the coven's Knower."

Ellie's hand dropped from the handle. To its detriment, the Portland coven didn't have a Knower, but she knew how the gift worked, how easily Rocky's thoughts of her would be extracted from his mind. More importantly, she knew how revered Knowers were, how closely protected.

"Which means you also live with Darian, the Regan." It was the only place a Knower would have the proper protection and provide the best service to the coven. "When you said the truck was your boss's—did you mean him, or the lead warrior?" Who also traditionally lived on the property with the Regan to provide security and advisement. Her voice betrayed her panic. There was no way her secret would stay safe. How could she possibly have any worse luck?

"I won't tell them about you."

"You won't have a choice!"

"They won't ask if they don't have to—if I don't show up where I'm not supposed to be, in front of three witnesses from the coven. They don't want to know. They can't know. As long as I don't flaunt it, as long as nothing like tonight ever happens again, I'm pretty sure they'll turn a blind eye."

"Pretty sure? Is that supposed to be reassuring? How did this happen? Why didn't you tell me right away?"

"For the same reason you're not telling me your

whole story, I imagine." He gave her time to deny it, but she didn't. "I thought you were safer not knowing. Look, I'll explain all of it, but you're right, there's no time tonight. Can I see you again?"

Ellie didn't know what to say. She had been so abhorred by what she thought was merely self-preservation back in the alley. Then she'd been forced to consider that he had been trying to help her—against everything he was trained to do. Now she was furious he'd kept so much from her, despite knowing how hypocritical that was.

And then there was his unfinished statement. The female he…what? Fed from? Cared about? Loved? That was crazy. He hardly knew her. And the first time he didn't act exactly as she hoped, she'd thrown the book at him.

"I'm working next Tuesday."

"I'm not waiting until next Tuesday. And I'm not having this conversation at a bar crawling with humans. I'll come back tomorrow or the next day when they're asleep. I'll explain. Then you can decide. But as I told you that first night, I'll keep your secret, no matter what."

Ellie only nodded. She was afraid if she opened her mouth, she'd tell him not to bother. Or she'd invite him in to stay and hide indefinitely with her.

Ellie hadn't really expected Rocky to show up the next day. She figured he'd want to lay low for a few hours at least. She was glad. She needed a few hours herself to sort through her feelings. Part of her hoped he wouldn't return to tell his story, that he would realize he'd risked too much already and stay away. But even after only a few nights of being with him, she knew that was unlikely. So the other part of her almost hoped he had gotten caught.

That would be easier for both of them. The decision would be taken out of their hands.

Rocky, however, had never been clear about what getting caught would mean for him. Would it be a slap on the wrist reprimand? Would he, like she, be sent back to his family? Or was it something else, something worse? Ellie had replayed the events of the other night enough to see what she had originally missed due to her own fear. When Rocky had retreated back to their hiding place after seeing his coven's warriors, he had appeared as terrified as she had felt. The image of his fear-stricken face resurfaced in her memory more than once over the next two days. Whether he'd admit it or not, that look was rooted in something deeper than whatever fear he had of *her* getting caught—even if he had fallen for her, as she suspected he had.

By Friday morning his fearful expression was all she could think about. As noon approached and there was still no sign of him, she made a difficult decision. If Rocky didn't show up that day, she would present herself to the Regan at the coven's club that night and demand to know what happened to him. Being an important member of a sister coven, she doubted she'd be denied. She also doubted she'd be allowed to stay. Finally, she forced herself to admit what had been creeping into her consciousness over the last three days. Without Rocky, she wasn't sure she wanted to stay.

Still in pajama bottoms and a cable knit sweater, Ellie forced herself off the futon where she had spent the better part of each day staring out the window at the street. She grabbed a fresh set of clothes from the suitcase she was still living out of and was heading to the bathroom when she caught a flash of white. The Regan's truck was parked outside the building.

"What happened? What took you so long?" she asked opening the door for him. She realized she had given herself away as his tense shoulders relaxed. He didn't exactly grin, but there was less intensity to his gaze.

"I'm fine. I just live with a bunch of insomniacs. When the Regan's not pacing his office all night, the lead warrior's out in the barn taking out his frustration on a dime-sized knot in the wood with half a dozen throwing knives." Rocky had walked into the small ground-floor apartment and taken off his hat. He wrung it in his hands as his eyes scanned the open living room and tiny kitchen. His gaze had just landed on the bohemian-looking bed sheet Talia had hung as wall art when Ellie refocused him.

"So they still don't know?"

Rocky snorted. "I'm not that naïve, and they're not that stupid."

She waited for him to explain.

"I told you the other night, they don't want to know. For now, at least. But they made it clear that would change if Tuesday was repeated."

Rocky collapsed onto the futon, which had been folded to its upright position, and recounted his too-close-for-comfort call.

Rocky stood at the top of the stairs leading from the basement to the main foyer of the farmhouse that was his new home. With one sleeve of his sweatshirt pulled over most of his hand to hide his obviously broken knuckles, he held the tray containing the dirty dishes from a dinner he could hardly touch. He tried to keep his nerves, and therefore, his hands steady, so that the clattering silverware wouldn't betray him. As he'd picked at his food, he had left ajar the door to the basement bedroom he'd been given, knowing the conversation would lead to the night's attack. Sarah had held dinner an hour until Markus, Sage, and Darian had returned from the warrior's meeting Markus had hastily called after being informed of the incident. He expected she'd want an explanation. Sure enough, they had begun to rehash it for her a few minutes ago, assuring her the young male would make a full and speedy recovery. His broken arm had been set and the young female he'd been feeding from had already provided him the essence he needed to heal, much to his doting mother's chagrin.

"If his own mother is more concerned with his boner than his broken bone, there's no need for you to worry," Sage told Sarah, who sighed at the crass remark.

"Sage." Darian was glaring at him. Rocky expected him to apologize immediately. The Knower merely shrugged.

"You can come in, Rocky." Sarah was wiping her hands on a dishtowel, having finished washing the rest of the dinner dishes.

Rocky was told, when he first began serving his sentence, that his dinners would be made for him, so long as he ate them in his room and cleaned up after himself. Having no experience with cooking, he had been thrilled with the deal. Having to perform the domestic duty in front of the three males who usually lingered in the kitchen over a couple beers, however, was a little degrading. Then again, he supposed that was the whole point of his punishment. He hoped, after a century or so, it would get easier.

He didn't look at the Regan, his lead warrior, or Rocky's new trainer and partner on patrols, the coven's Knower, as he made his way to the sink with the tray. Sarah smiled at him warmly as she left, a smile he found difficult to return.

He was relieved when the males resumed talking, until he discovered they hadn't changed the subject.

"So you've shifted more patrols to the area for awhile?" Darian asked Markus.

"Yeah."

Rocky grinned, washing his glass for the third time as he eavesdropped. The more patrols near Ellie's home and work, the better.

"Something funny, kid?"

Rocky's head jerked up at being addressed. At twenty-three, compared to their nearly nine hundred years combined experience, he would be 'kid' for quite some time. Realizing Sage had been watching him in the reflection of the kitchen window behind the sink, Rocky swallowed the swears he aimed at himself and tried to look collected. He placed the glass on the drying rack very deliberately before turning around.

"No, I just…wish we had been on patrols tonight." Rocky had been out with Sage half a dozen nights already. The most they'd done is escort various coven females from their work back to their cars or homes.

"And do you wish you were the warrior who needed seventeen stitches to sew up the gash in his thigh or the one who's got three broken ribs? Because I can arrange either."

"Markus." Darian shook his head at his lead warrior.

Rocky didn't bother to mutter an apology. It was shit luck that the lead warrior had been Sage's partner the night six months ago when the Knower had to be called to cover for him. Rocky had gotten into a fight at a human bar and accidentally sprung his fangs, terrifying some co-eds whom he'd caught slipping something into a girl's drink. Sage made sure *they* didn't remember it. Markus had spent the last month making it clear to Rocky that *he* remembered it well. He'd pegged Rocky that night as a mouthy, spoiled punk. Rocky figured it'd likely take him the better part of his sentence to convince Markus otherwise—if that could be done.

Rocky was wiping his hands on his jeans, ready to head back to his room when Sage dropped their three beer glasses in the sink. Rocky knew he was expected to wash them and started on it without saying a word. Markus and Darian were already heading for the foyer, no doubt to continue their conversation in privacy, from him, up in the Regan's home office. But Sage remained leaning on the counter watching Rocky. The young male was never as quick a learner as his father demanded, but he wasn't thick. He had lived with Sage over a month and worked with him for a week. He knew the Knower was waiting for him to look up and make eye contact. There was no way Rocky was letting him in his head tonight.

"You know, kid, maybe you *can* help with what went down tonight."

"Sure, you and I can go hunt and kill a few Vengatti tomorrow night." Rocky never looked up as he put the last glass on the counter to dry, but when he turned, Sage shoved his hand under Rocky's nose. In it was an empty bullet casing.

"One of the Vengatti was killed by a clean headshot seconds before Nicolo and Sean arrived. They heard the shot come from the other side of the street. Had to be one hell of a marksman to hit a moving vampire from that distance. Seems strange whoever it was didn't stick around or come forward afterwards. The coven gives awards for crap like that, right?"

Sage knew damn well Rocky had won every coven competition for marksmanship since he was fourteen. He especially excelled at hitting moving targets. That and his reputation as an uncontrolled, but tough fighter were part of what convinced Markus to grant him a trial period working with the warriors. Well, those and a hope he'd get himself badly injured, Rocky surmised.

Sage grabbed Rocky's uninjured hand. "You're a gun guy. What can you tell us about it?"

As soon as he dropped the casing into Rocky's hand, Rocky pulled back, breaking contact. His heart rate increased when he glanced across the kitchen to see the Regan and lead warrior had stopped to hear his reply.

"Someone got lucky—Justin from the sounds of it." He named the young victim, who had been presented the same fateful night as Rocky's sister, Maria. "What's there to tell?"

"The gun?" Sage asked dryly.

Rocky rolled the casing in his cupped palm. "Looks like this was off a forty-five hollow point. Dozens of guns can fire that."

"Most common among coven members is a Beretta, though, right? Like the ones you and your father owned?"

Rocky wanted to glare at him. He wanted to search his face for the confirmation of his greatest fear. Sage was making him sweat on purpose. And why? If he wanted to accuse him, he could have done it the minute they arrived home. Rocky wouldn't have denied it. He wouldn't outright lie to the three males who saved him from being beaten to death by his own coven members, despite the trouble it caused them. If the point was to scare him, he was a little too late. Discovering he'd left behind the casing; knowing his scent, made stronger by the trash, blood, and gunpowder, was not only in the alley, but all over the Regan's truck; and nearly being caught by Sarah sneaking a first aid kit into his room had left his knees knocking for hours. He was pretty sure he'd survived the worst of the evening. Sage's questioning was becoming more frustrating than frightening.

Rocky finally looked up. "I guess. They're reliable weapons. But good luck finding the shooter based on that or this." He held up the spent casing. Darian and Markus were still watching. The lead warrior eyed him with suspicion that left Rocky wondering if he, too, could read minds. Rocky couldn't give him what he wanted, but he could give him what he expected: mouthy punk.

"I don't suppose I'll be getting the newest model now that I'm working with the warriors?"

"Good supposition," Markus sneered before heading up the stairs.

Darian shot Rocky a look. "Careful, kid."

"Sorry, Regan." But he wasn't too sorry, because it had worked. He hadn't wanted to cross the line, just to nudge it enough that they'd temporarily forget why they'd originally been focused on him.

The Regan nodded and flashed up the stairs after Markus.

"Here." Rocky tried to give the casing back to Sage.

"Keep it. Consider it an early birthday present." Sage reached over and squeezed Rocky's fist over the shell. His crushing grip made the message clear. Still Rocky tried to act innocent and not show his pain as Sage squeezed tighter.

"My birthday was last week."

"I know. I meant for next year and the year after that."

And the decade or two after that, I suppose.

"Good supposition," Sage echoed Markus in response to Rocky's thought. He gave a final squeeze that left Rocky wondering if he'd be able to use either hand come the next evening. "And, kid, if you're stupid enough to keep it, find a better place than your sock drawer. Next time, that broken hand is going to feel like a Swedish massage."

Rocky could only nod. He had no idea if Sage was referring to the hand he'd just crushed or the one Rocky had punched into the brick wall. But the rest of the message was clear. There was only one thing other than tube socks and boxers in his sock drawer: the Beretta whose magazine, missing just one round, was filled with ammo matching the case in his hand.

"So why are you here?" Ellie was starting to wonder if Rocky had suicidal tendencies.

"I told you, I need to tell you the truth—all of it. Besides, I don't think Sage was telling me not to see you. He was warning me not to be seen. The gun's hidden now. I'll go without it for a few months, I guess."

She didn't comment that a few months wasn't nearly long enough to fade the memories of the older vamps with whom he was living. She'd seen enough other warriors with their weapons to know that, for Rocky, leaving the house without his gun likely felt like entering the coven's club wearing only his fangs.

Ellie sat across from him in the battered papasan chair Talia had to have salvaged from the curb outside a college apartment last May. She crossed her legs and waited.

Rocky didn't hesitate before launching into the rest of his tale.

"First, you've got to understand I earned a reputation as a hothead right before and after I matured. Bar fights mostly."

"Shocking." She couldn't help but laugh. "The eldest son of a first family causing trouble?" The Portland coven was smaller, but there had been three other first family heirs about her brother's age. Together with her brother Nathan, the coven had taken to calling them the fearsome foursome because of all the havoc they caused. Eighteen-year-old boys should never be told that the world, or their world at least, would soon be theirs for the taking without any work to be done by them. It created a dangerous combination of power and youthful stupidity.

"Yeah, I know." Rocky grinned. "Only I always managed to get caught, not just by my father, but by the human cops. I've got my father's temper, but I tried to put it to good use. It just never went as planned."

"Defending females?" Ellie remembered how quickly he'd lost it in Murphy's when one of the girls was assaulted.

Rocky blushed and nodded. "As I mentioned, the last time was after I matured. It required the Knower in order to completely clean up. It was solely because of our status that my father and I weren't dragged in front of the Regan, but Markus, the lead warrior, made it very clear that next time there would be consequences. My dad was furious and humiliated by being dressed down by a mere warrior, but he wisely directed both these emotions my way. He promised Markus there wouldn't be a next time, that I'd seen the last of the human world for a long while."

"But there was a next time? Another bar brawl?"

"No. Not a bar fight. He kept his word on that. I wasn't allowed out of his sight for the next six months other than to sleep. And even that he made sure was uncomfortable, as I couldn't lay on my back for at least five of those six months."

Ellie winced, although she couldn't see her own father, or any prominent coven member, reacting much differently to such an incident.

"So if it wasn't in a human bar..." Ellie trailed off. She knew there were vampire-only establishments in Bristol, but surely at twenty-something Rocky hadn't picked a fight with a vampire older and stronger than he was, especially not a fight involving a spoken-for female.

Rocky seemed to read her expression. "It wasn't at a vampire bar either." He paused searching her face, bracing himself. "It was at this year's ball."

Ellie's jaw dropped. The Creator's Day ball was the biggest night of the year, a chance for families to flaunt their status, present their newly matured young, arrange matings, anything that could raise their reputation, all while pretending to honor the blessed Creator. No one ever visibly crossed the line at the ball. It was social suicide.

Rocky launched immediately into an explanation.

"I was charged with taking my sister home early. She was technically still a few days from maturing. Her fangs hadn't come in, but she and my mother had bullied my father into letting her be presented with the other new vamps so she wouldn't have to wait another year. Honestly, I don't think he would have agreed to it if he weren't still smarting from my fight the previous summer. He wanted as desperately as Maria to have the focus return to our family for a positive reason. So a little after midnight I showed up where we had agreed to meet. Only she wasn't there." Rocky ground his teeth remembering. "I heard her cry out from a room upstairs and crashed my way in. Another son of a first family was...on her."

Ellie put a hand over her mouth. She knew what Rocky had found.

"I don't know if he had already...raped her, or if he

was just about to. I didn't care. And I sure as hell didn't wait for a full confession." Rocky was staring at his bruised fist, still healing from Tuesday night.

"You attacked him."

He nodded.

"Good. He deserved it. Anyone ought to have agreed with that."

"They might have—if I hadn't completely lost it." Rocky locked eyes with her. "I crushed his fang."

Ellie had been expecting the worst. She expected him to say he killed him. This answer was unexpected but just as serious, perhaps more so. Injuring the fang of another male, particularly a young powerful male, was cause for execution in their world. The only thing that would excuse it would be defending another coven member, especially a female, from the kind of attack Rocky had just described. But having to face the coven after sustaining such an injury, for such a reason, would ruin the other male's reputation—something beyond value for a first family heir. Any male of that status would make whatever denial or counter accusation necessary to maintain a shred of dignity. Rocky must have known from her gasp that he needn't explain that.

"But your sister?"

"Was in shock. Was afraid of being punished for presenting herself before her time. Was traumatized by what that asshole had done or attempted to."

"It's been two months now."

"It doesn't matter." Rocky was wringing his hat again. "The sentence has already been agreed to."

"*Your* sentence."

Rocky nodded again. "The other male denied everything. Said I had walked in on he and Maria having a consensual and innocuous tryst and freaked. Maria agreed or at least wouldn't speak up to disagree. My father, a coven lawyer mind you, walked into that hotel room and quite quickly realized he had a choice. He could risk everything fighting for a son whom half the coven had already written off as a bad egg, or he could walk away virtually unscathed. He'd lose a pain-in-the-ass son, but Maria's reputation could be salvaged by letting her attacker's story become the truth the coven would be told. And he'd look like the self-sacrificing coven member of the century, willing to hand over his only heir in the name of justice for the greater good."

"I don't understand. Your coven has a Knower. Even if no one would believe you, he could prove you innocent—or justified, at least."

Rocky shook his head. "First families have the right of refusal. The other male's father claimed it'd be too traumatic while he healed to have the Knower resurface and read the memory of that night. My father employed the same excuse for Maria's behalf, or so he said."

"Figures. Why let a little thing like the truth get in the way of our power or reputations?" Ellie spat. "What about *your* memories, though?"

Rocky shrugged. "My father had already disowned me. He wasn't about to take that back. I couldn't risk Maria being seen as damaged goods. Now she's the only child of an heirless first family. Every second and third born son of a future Elder will want to mate her, knowing her son will eventually have a place on the Elder Council."

How twisted was their world that these were the things Rocky had considered while facing his own death sentence?

"Then how'd you get off?"

"Get off?" Rocky scoffed. "I'm serving a two

hundred year sentence as the Regan's gofer boy to pay off the family of the male I injured. I lost my family, my name, whatever reputation I had left. I hardly consider that getting off."

Ellie understood his misplaced anger, but that didn't mean she had to tolerate it.

"You know what I mean. Without justification, the sentence for what you did is usually death."

He took a steadying breath to regain control. "I eventually let the Knower read my memory after Darian promised he'd do his best to keep what happened to Maria from becoming general knowledge. I hadn't seen enough of Maria's attack to prove anything definitively, but it was enough to convince the Regan to fight for a lesser sentence. It took him weeks and made him pretty unpopular with some of the Elders. I nearly died from a lack of essence waiting for an agreement. But he forced their hand, finally. He fed me himself the night he came into the cell to release me into his custody. I owe him my life, literally. So you were right: you weren't my only reason for not stepping forward to help the other night. It's one thing for my housemates to suspect I'm leaving to feed. It'd be another if two warriors and a young male saw me. It'd get out to the coven. I'd be in loads trouble, for sure, but Darian would take even more heat, which he certainly doesn't deserve."

"You respect him that deeply?" She couldn't help but think about her own Regan, her father, and wonder if any of his subjects felt that strongly about him. Her issues with him were personal. She had never stopped to think about how the rest of her coven viewed him.

"My father took the easiest path. Darian chose to do what was right, even though it was harder. I respect those kinds of decisions more than anything. That was why I snarled at you the other night. I'm sorry I reacted so strongly, but I don't ever want to be compared to the male formerly known as my father."

Ellie giggled at his attempt at humor. Not that it was all that funny. It was just nice to see he maintained it through everything he'd just told her about.

"I understand that. I understand most of it, actually." And she did. She realized she had been wrong to judge him so quickly the other night. "The thing I don't understand is why, if you respect him so much, you'd risk leaving at all."

Rocky stuck a thumb between his teeth to bite at what little nail he had left.

"I shouldn't," he finally answered. "I waited two weeks after the Regan first fed me, thinking some arrangement would be made. When I couldn't wait any longer, I snuck out. I don't know what I was thinking. The chances of finding someone willing to feed me were slim to nonexistent. And I guess I knew that if I outright asked one of them, someone would have fed me. But the thought of having another male feed me because I couldn't sustain my own strength…"

"Would be like getting kicked in the nuts every week?"

"Ellie!" His tone reminded her of her mother, but the laughter that followed was all Rocky.

"I have a brother. I unfortunately know all too well how males your age think."

"Yeah, well, maybe I would've come around to the idea eventually, but then I found you." His gaze was intense again, all humor evaporated. "Mad Murphy's was the third bar I'd gone into that night. At that point I was ready to down a drink and head back to the Regan's. Finding you was both terrifying and—"

"Lucky," she interrupted, not sure if she was ready to hear his whole answer.

"Amazing," he finished anyway. "Ellie, you never answered my question the other night, and I suppose even if you had, you might have changed your mind since. Do you still want this?"

Despite her doubt and her anger over the last two days, she'd thought about this. She was ready for this question.

"No."

She watched as Rocky sucked in a breath and then tried to hide it. He stood quickly and put back on his hat, pulling it low to hide his expression.

"Okay. I understand." He started for the door.

"No, you don't," Ellie laughed as she crawled out of the over-sized chair and flashed in front of him. "I don't want to do *this* anymore, what we've been doing, exchanging essence in alleys and then walking away for the rest of the week. But that's not what you want either, is it?"

His chin sank to his chest. "I can't have what I want with you, a normal relationship."

"Yeah, well, normal's over-rated. Meanwhile, dangerous and secretive sound pretty enticing." She ran a fingernail down his chest, so slowly it seemed to pain him as his gaze followed its progress. She stopped at his waistband, which he wore low on his hips.

"Even if it's only one night a week?" he whispered pulling her into him.

"Anticipation makes everything more intense," she breathed into his neck. "Which is why you're going to have to wait until Tuesday." She kissed his check then shoved him away.

"What?" He sounded like a little boy who had his

balloon popped. Ellie couldn't help but laugh at him.

"Talia'll be home to get ready for work anytime now. And since I spent the first half of the day waiting for you and trying to decide what to wear when I barged into your coven's club demanding to know what happened to you, I really need a shower before my shift starts, preferably one with hot water, which I won't have if Talia takes hers first. So, go. Scat." She had already opened the door for him.

"You were going to the club? Are you serious?"

"Not as serious as I am about you needing to leave."

Rocky was allowing her to push him into the hallway, but when she went to close the door, he jammed his boot between the door and the frame. He seemed to have recovered from the last few minutes.

"Are you happy here?"

Hadn't she just admitted she wanted to stay because of him?

"I mean in this apartment." Rocky was gesturing to the room he'd just been ejected from.

"As you can imagine, it lacks some of the comforts of home, but it's cheap. And if it means I can be free, then I'm willing to live without a closet for awhile."

"On the ground floor? Without an alarm? With a main door that can be shaken open, even when everyone remembers to lock it?"

Ellie found she wasn't bothered knowing he'd tried. She had taken note of all these things when she moved in, but what could she do?

"It's worth the risk, at least until I can afford something better."

Rocky nodded, but she could see his wheels spinning. Once again his need to play the hero was sexy, but not if it led to some crazy plan that'd get them both caught. She leaned in and kissed him. It wasn't the dismissive peck on the cheek her prior kiss had been. It was wanton, lingering, inviting a response from him that took his mind fully off the topic of security. And when she nudged his boot aside and shut the door on his lustful look, it was cruel.

And, as the sigh he released from the other side of the door confirmed, it was hot. Very hot.

Lauren Grimley

7. Special Victims Unit: Part 4

"How PG, even for a princess," Vivian commented when it became clear Ellie would not continue. They had all been listening intently, waiting for her to finish.

Alex shook her head as her sense confirmed why Ellie cut her story short. "It's not the sex she's withholding. She still doesn't trust me to keep from Sage and Markus whatever it was that came next."

"Maybe I would trust you, if you'd spoken up however long ago it was that those two showed up outside the door."

Alex realized she was the only one still looking at Ellie. As she refocused her sense, she knew why. She cringed as she turned around to confirm that Rocky and Sage were standing in the open doorway. Rocky looked pale, Sage furious, an emotion she began to mirror when she realized he had stopped blocking her, pulling who knows what from her head. Would she ever make a lasting truce with Elizabeth?

"Whatever you heard, from Ellie's story or my

thoughts, forget it. Ellie was telling it in confidence to us; our connection doesn't give you the right to break the promise we all made her." Alex stood so Sage could see her clearly. She wanted there to be no doubt that she was deadly serious.

"As you so kindly clarified, she never got far enough in her story for your thoughts to be of any use. His thoughts, however, need a little explanation." Sage shoved Rocky into the room by his neck.

Rocky glanced at Ellie, clearly frustrated she had shared what she had. "When you started to mention Talia's apartment, I thought—well, I thought, and that's a problem around Sage." Rocky turned on Alex. "Not all of us have the luxury of blocking him."

Alex wanted to tell him that anytime he wanted to trade *luxuries*, she'd be more than happy to pass off her gift. She knew, though, that his anger wasn't really aimed at her. Admittedly, that *was* a luxury of her gift.

"For once, short stuff isn't to blame." Sage turned to Ellie. "She was too intent on picking apart your emotions to feel us outside. She's used to sensing us enough that she doesn't always register it."

Alex presumed this was his way of helping her smooth things over with Ellie. She wasn't sure it did her any favors.

"Go on, Rocky, finish the story. Your adoring fans are dying to hear how it ends."

"Sage." Sarah stood and shot him a cold look.

"He's going to tell it at some point tonight, Sarah. Better here than in Darian's office. If you don't like it, leave."

Sarah flashed to within inches of him. Vivian shook her head, apparently used to other females reprimanding her partner.

"You speak to me like that again, Knower, and you'll be the only one accounting for yourself to the Regan. Is that understood?"

Alex wondered if he was cocky enough to defy her, but she sensed the humiliation his blushless face hid.

"Fine."

Sarah waited.

Vivian whispered in a singsong voice, "Not an apology."

Sage took a second to glare at his partner before meeting Sarah's eyes again.

"Sorry." He waited until Sarah nodded and stepped back before he started to the door.

"Wait."

All eyes turned back to Rocky who had made his way to Ellie's chair. He sat on the arm holding one of her hands in his own.

"He heard enough of it. I might as well tell him. It's not as bad as what these ladies are probably thinking I did."

Suddenly Vivian slapped her thigh and let out a tinkling laugh that left everyone staring.

"You used his credit card to rent her a safer apartment." Vivian's amusement over this was obvious, if unexpected.

"Um, yeah, well, his and Markus's." Rocky paused expecting Vivian to explain how she knew. When she didn't, he blundered on. "When they discovered I was good with computers, they had me transfer a lot of their accounts. Online billing and banking were safer, more anonymous than P.O. boxes in the city, which someone had to empty frequently. They had to give me all their account information, though." Rocky paused to suck in a breath. "I funneled the amount of half her rent from each of their accounts into an online bill-pay for her."

Sage growled, but he wasn't looking at Rocky. He was eying Vivian, who continued to giggle.

"The credit card you used was the one Sage has for me. So when the company called to make sure the charges were legitimate, it went to my cell," she explained. "He's pissed I didn't tell him. Or because I didn't speak to or feed him for nearly a month afterwards with no explanation."

"Or both," Sage interjected.

"In fairness, I thought you had another female on the side. A mysterious apartment on the other side of Bristol? What would you have thought?"

"I wouldn't have thought. I would have asked." Anyone who hadn't spent a century staring into them would have broken under the stormy glare of Sage's grey eyes.

Vivian simply rolled her own. "Right. You mean you would have pulled it from my mind. Not the same."

"So how'd you figure out he didn't—have another female, I mean?" Alex butted in, hoping to stave off a major argument.

"When Markus complained about having to feed him. He wouldn't have asked Markus if he had a bimbo on the side. I figured the apartment was for—" Vivian stopped when Sage spun on her. "Someone else," she finished with a sigh. Alex sensed there was more to it, but that was a mystery for another day. Rocky continued to explain.

"You know I'd never have stolen from you or Markus, if—"

"Rocky," Alex tried to cut him off.

"Shut up, twerp."

She spun on Sage, but it was too late. Darian and Markus had already entered. What little color had returned to Rocky's face, drained instantly.

"Please, finish." Darian joined the others in the seating area, his arms crossed, his eyes never leaving his shaking young warrior.

Markus's gaze moved between Alex, who was pleading with her expression for him to remain calm, and Rocky, whom he eyed with suspicion after catching the last snippet of conversation.

"If it hadn't been absolutely necessary, I think he was about to say," Alex jumped in. "And it was, of course, because even after Ellie came forward, no one in the coven thought to see to her safety, except Rocky. Both of you can afford the loss of a few months' rent. After all, you didn't even notice it was missing from your accounts. And considering all that Ellie went through, it'd be rather petty of you to ask for her and Rocky to repay it. Think of it as a charitable donation to the SVC."

"The what?" Markus asked. Alex tried not to look too pleased with herself and her gift when she heard only curiosity in his voice.

"The Sassy Vixens' Club," Vivian answered right on cue. "Which, by the way, has female-only membership requirements, not to mention, by the Regan's own orders, exclusive use of this wing." She turned to Darian.

"I...we...it was getting late. Rocky and Sage were supposed to get you all." Darian, too, seemed to have 'forgotten' his anger.

"We got side-tracked," Sage spat. "Not unlike this conversation." He had moved to stand over Alex, who thankfully still sat next to Vivian on the loveseat. Alex hadn't bothered to try to influence Sage. His gift made him virtually immune to this part of her power, and it only further irritated him if she attempted to surpass it.

The tiny dark-haired vampire reached back and patted

her lover's chest. "Let it go, babe. Trust me, it'll be better for all involved." When she tugged at his waistband, the look he gave her was half fury, half arousal.

"O-kay," Alex drew out the word in disgust. "I think Darian's right. It's time to call it quits for tonight." Alex was the first one to her feet.

"Just for tonight?" Markus asked. Alex felt, more than saw, the others waiting for her reply.

"Yeah. I'll come back next week, but don't think that gets you off the hook for planning this behind my back," she warned her mate. In the short silence that followed, she sensed the collective relief and satisfaction. Blush began creeping up her neck.

Forever her savior, Vivian leaned over and whispered, rather loudly for a vampire, "I can lend you our paddle, if you'd like."

A cacophony of disgusted moans and amused chuckles filled the room, but it got the others moving, not to mention diverted their thoughts far from the two previous conversations.

Sage was apparently threatening to do any number of nasty things to Vivian, all of which seemed to entice her. Darian helped Sarah off the couch, resting his hand ever so briefly on her belly. Rocky waited nervously as Markus with Cormelia, and then Darian with Sarah walked by without so much as a dirty look. He then gave Ellie a quick, relieved peck on the forehead.

Alex still worried about the males' slightly glassy stares, but Sarah and Cormelia's grins put her more at ease. Even more comforting was what she sensed from Ellie, who stood silently at Rocky's side. She hadn't spoken since accusing Alex of not stopping her story in time, but Alex was confident that Ellie knew and appreciated what Alex had just done. Alex had meant what she said about protecting Rocky, and Ellie was starting to believe it. For that reason alone, there was hope they'd someday find common ground, at the very least, if not a lasting friendship.

"Thank you," Rocky whispered when the others were in the hall.

"For what?" Alex smirked.

"That wasn't your most subtle work, Seer." Sage stopped, despite Vivian's tug on his arm. "We'll see how pleased you are halfway through dinner when one of them snaps out of it, and you and Rocky both end up in the cell in the basement."

"I wouldn't let that happen, if I were you, Knower," Vivian said not bothering to keep her own voice down. "Especially since you haven't fed in nearly a week. Another two or three could seem like a very long time." She patted his chest and with a wink headed into the hall. Sage paused only long enough to flash his fangs at Alex and Rocky before following her like a very large, very feral dog on a seriously short leash. Alex, Rocky, and Ellie wisely avoided making eye contact as they silently trod behind the others.

"Speaking of eating," Darian said to Sarah, his mind obviously still slightly muddled from Alex's hasty work, "did Diane say what she's making us for dinner?"

The temptation too great, Alex couldn't help but turn to Ellie with a grin. They might never be friends, but they shared certain qualities. Ellie knew exactly what the Seer was thinking, and at the same time both blurted it out.

"Lamb stew?"

Despite Sarah's glare, Alex and Ellie filled the otherwise empty hallway with a chorus of girlish giggles neither still believed the other or herself capable of. For at least as long as their laughter lasted, they weren't anyone's enemies, or subjects, or victims. They weren't lashed to a past they'd rather forget, or fretting about a future in which the only certainty was more adversity. They were simply two young females sharing a moment of unbridled joy.

GLOSSARY

Council of Elders – The male heads of the first families who form a governing/advisory council. While final decisions are left to the Regan, they still hold sway both with him and the rest of the coven due to their wealth and status.

Creator – The deity worshipped by the vampires, depicted as a virginal female who created both humans and vampires. It is believed the Creator wanted there to be a balance to everything. Gifts are balanced with dangers, like a Seer's maturity. Strength is balanced with vulnerabilities, like the vampires losing their ability to be out in daylight beyond the lifespan of a human (around eighty to hundred years).

Creator's Day – A day of the year set aside to give thanks to the Creator, celebrated on the winter solstice, the longest night of the year and therefore the night vampires have the most freedom for which to thank the Creator. The celebration begins at midnight and lasts through noon. Traditionally Rectinatti vampires wear white and silver on the holiday. Silver symbolizes the coven; white represents the purity of the Creator. Decorations include a wreath of moonflower with a silver dagger placed in the center. The flower, a white, night blooming flower which, although beautiful, is poisonous, represents the females or protectors. The dagger symbolizes the males or warriors.

Dia dhuit/Dia is Muire dhuit – Irish greetings literally translated to "may God bless you" and "may God and Mary bless you." The Rectinatti adopted them shortly after moving to Ireland to blend in with the locals, but also because the Irish revered and depicted the Virgin Mary in ways similar to how the vampires viewed their Creator. The greeting and response is still used formally, especially on Creator's Day, to show respect and reverence to the one being addressed, as well as to the Creator.

Elder Regan – A living male who served as Regan, but has since stepped aside for his son.

essence – The substance carried in one's blood that holds his or her spirit or life energy. Essence encapsulates all that is good about a vampire or person. Without a certain amount of essence one is left conscienceless. Vampires need to draw essence from another to maintain their enhanced strength and speed. The Rectinatti exchange essence with their mates or family members. The Vengatti drain essence from humans. An average vampire can't live more than four or five weeks without another's essence.

First Families – Families who can claim a pure bloodline, with no members having ever fed from humans. There are about a dozen first families (each with multiple generations) in the Bristol coven. Most first families have both status and wealth. Since mating outside a first family would taint the bloodline, it is frowned upon for all and absolutely forbidden of first-born sons.

Knower – A vampire who can hear others' thoughts and manipulate their memories. Most of the time this requires eye-contact or physical touch, but the thoughts of those with whom a Knower becomes close can often be heard anywhere within a relatively short distance (up to a half mile). Knowing is considered a gift granted by the Creator because of the importance of this power to a coven. Knowers are usually males and are marked with two scar-like lines in their brows. The gift, which develops shortly after they mature into adult vampires, is not necessarily hereditary, but can be.

mate – The vampire equivalent of husband or wife. Mating ceremonies are much like marriage ceremonies, except for the essence exchange and the cleansing ritual, which takes place the night before. Matings are for eternity. Only if one loses a mate prior to having young can he/she mate again by first undergoing a renewal ritual.

Rectinatti – The coven of vampires who believe in a balance of power between humans and vampires. They feed exclusively from other vampires and work to protect humans from becoming the prey of the Vengatti.

> **History:** Originally there was one Rectinatti coven residing in Italy. Most then moved to Ireland in the late 1500s to escape the Vengatti, who learned the locations of the Regan and first families through a traitor. When the Vengatti were forced to leave Ireland in the 1840s due to the famine killing off their food source (humans), the Rectinatti followed them to assure the safety of the humans in their new home, America. The majority of both covens settled in Bristol, MA, although smaller groups formed their own covens in other areas of the US and Canada, currently Portland and Vancouver.

> **Facts:** The coven is led by a Regan, a position passed on through bloodlines to the first-born male. The Regan is advised by the Council of Elders, a group consisting of the male head of each of the coven's first families. The Regan and males of first families wear a ring of sapphire and silver to symbolize their status and their pure heritage.

Regan – The leader of a coven. Both Vengatti and Rectinatti covens have Regans. The position is passed on through a family to the oldest male. A Regan ascends when his father steps aside or dies.

returning (ceremony) – When one has served his/her coven, raised young, and lived a full life, one can choose to return to the Creator. In the vampire world, this is not suicide. Such ceremonies honor the life of the one returning; they're dignified and accepted, just as the passing of elders ought to be.

Seer – A human with the gift of being able to sense and sometimes manipulate others' emotions. Seers have traditionally always been males; Alex is the exception to this. Their gift is hereditary and matures to full strength sometime around twenty, a process many don't survive due to the physical toll it takes on one's body. Over history, different Seers have developed different powers to varying degrees, all related to affecting others' emotions. Seers age slower, develop stronger essence, and heal quicker than average humans, possibly allowing them to live as long as vampires. No one knows for sure, because no Seer has ever died a natural death.

Vengatti (sometimes referred to as the Others by the Rectinatti) – The opposing coven of vampires who split from the Rectinatti back in Italy. The Vengatti believed that humans were growing too quickly in numbers and strength and resented having to live in secrecy from them. Feeling they were the superior race, the Vengatti began to feed from humans rather than each other. Because humans have less essence and it is not an exchange, feeding from them often leaves them unable to recover, rendering them conscienceless.

Also by Lauren Grimley

From the Alex Crocker series:
Unforeseen, **book 1**
Hunted for her gift. Haunted by her dreams. Driven to fight.

Alex was quite sure *gifted* was a term delusional parents applied to their strictly average children, *vampires* were gorgeous dead guys in her eighth-grade girls' novels, and *Seers* was a middle schooler's misspelling of a department store known for power tools. Teachers, however, don't know everything—it's Alex's turn to be educated.

Unveiled, **book 2**
With strength comes vulnerabilities. With love comes loss. With power comes pain. The world Alex now belongs to hinges on such balance. However, her every step seems to be lurching her precariously closer to one wrong side or another.

As the strength of her gift begins to unveil itself, Alex needs to learn to control it—before it consumes her and endangers those she loves.

Unknown (a short story from the series)
Middle school is supposed to bite. Middle schoolers aren't.

Neither teacher nor student expected to glance across a classroom of normal human teenagers and into the face of their enemy. Neither Seer nor Knower could have understood how their gifts would leave them second-guessing everything they'd been taught to believe about the other side.

ABOUT THE AUTHOR

Lauren Grimley lives in central Massachusetts where she grew up, but her heart is on the beaches of Cape Cod where she spends as much of her time as possible. After graduating from Boston University she became a middle school English teacher. She now balances writing, reading, and correcting, all with a cat on her lap and a glass of red wine close by.

Unforeseen, the first novel in the Alex Crocker Seer series, was Lauren's debut novel. She has since continued the series with *Unveiled*, book two, and now *Unbridled*. To learn more about her or her writing or to connect with her online visit her website at www.laurengrimley.com.

www.ingramcontent.com/pod-product-compliance
Lightning Source LLC
Chambersburg PA
CBHW050940120626
46552CB00001B/304

* 9 7 8 0 6 1 5 8 6 1 1 1 1 *